Francis William Lauderdale Adams

Tiberius

Francis William Lauderdale Adams

Tiberius

ISBN/EAN: 9783337335267

Printed in Europe, USA, Canada, Australia, Japan

Cover: Foto ©Andreas Hilbeck / pixelio.de

More available books at **www.hansebooks.com**

TIBERIUS: A DRAMA
BY FRANCIS ADAMS

WITH INTRODUCTION
BY W. M. ROSSETTI

LONDON: T. FISHER UNWIN
PATERNOSTER SQUARE 1894

TO

HARRY BEARDOE ADAMS,

ONLY BROTHER—TRUEST CRITIC—DEAREST FRIEND,

WHO DIED AT STRADBROKE ISLAND,

MORETON BAY, QUEENSLAND,

13TH SEPT. 1892.

What he thought was my best—my strongest and most sincere,—this I give to him now, with all the unspeakable memories of our childhood, youth, and early manhood—to him whose strength was in his sincerity, and whose sincerity was sweeter to me than all strength.

ATQUE IN PERPETUUM, FRATER, AVE
ATQUE VALE!

HELOUAN, EGYPT,
New Year, 1893.

Up in the pallid and changeless blue
The intolerable sun
Blazes and burns.   For leagues and leagues,
Brown and billowless, the sea of grass
Stretches away.
Not a sound, not a movement anywhere !
Even the fiery locust is mute :
Even the tireless circling kite
Perches and sits on the withered bough :
Even the magpies, gathered together
Among the bottle-tree's shady leaves,
Gurgle no more.
Along the streaming horizon line
The haze-smoke flickers.   The mirage trees
Baseless stand beneath the hills
That hem round the north, all dim and blue.
Not a sound, not a movement anywhere !

Rise once more, O passionate shapes,
Haunters of my mind those seven long years :
Rise in the lonely place where alone I lie
Under the lovely withered oleander
In this forlorn and desolate garden !
Here where the long grass chokes the vines,
Where the strangling weeds oppress the faint flowers,
Where the creepers clutch and kill the fruit trees,
Where the jessamined arbours like a ruined house
Are pierced with the sun-shafts—
Rise, proud piteous terrible Face,
Startling ghost of my brooding boyhood,
Man and Lover, Emperor and Scourge,
Speak to me once again—
Touch my brain as you did when I knew you first—
Wring my heart till it feels yours beat ! . . .

I dream I see them !   All the shadowy Figures
Form and dissolve, while others, others
Take their places—
Eyes I have looked into, lips I have kissed,
Gaze and murmur and fade away.

JIMBOUR, QUEENSLAND DOWNS.
        New Year, 1889.

Introduction.

FRANCIS ADAMS, as some readers of this book will be aware, committed suicide in September last, before quite completing his thirtieth year; thus attaining just the same span of age as Shelley did. He was of a consumptive constitution; had gone on from bad to worse, suffered much, and knew there was no hope for him—only the prospect of still severer sufferings. His younger brother (to whom the drama of *Tiberius* is dedicated in a few touching words) had lately died, also of consumption, after enduring cruel pains from his inexorable disease. This, as I have understood, was one potent consideration in prompting the elder brother to linger no more, but take the matter into his own hands. He was not in the least mad, but determined and deliberate, although the British coroner's jury, with their usual lax indulgence, combined of good-nature and inability to place themselves in the suicide's point of view, brought in the accustomed verdict of "temporary insanity." There was no insanity ; if any there had been, it was not temporary, but spread over the morbid bodily conditions of several years, and the fully pondered train of thought arising out of those conditions.

Of Mr. Adams personally I knew very little. It may have been towards the middle of 1888 that he sent me by post from Australia the Australian edition of his *Songs of the Army of the Night*, with an inscription showing that he had paid attention to some of my writings, and was in sympathy with their tone upon certain points. Such a message from a man of whom I had never heard was a surprise to me, and a pleasant surprise. I at once read the book, and was genuinely astonished at its intensity and fierceness of tone, its depth of emotion, and its splendid instantaneousness of poetic perception, suggestion, and expression—

an instantaneousness as of lightning at twilight, revealing at one moment every corner and cranny of the scene, and at the next moment plunging all into a more sombre obscurity than before : the inarticulate things of passion and of poetry hurtled upon the mind through the articulate. Though far from blind to the excesses of opinion and of feeling in the volume, or to its defects as well as excesses of diction, I thought it one of the most remarkable and moving of recent poetic productions, and I wrote at once to the author to say as much. We then exchanged one or two further letters, and I looked through his earlier book named *Poetical Works*. When he came to London in September 1890, I saw him once, and regretted that it should be only once. I found him to be a young man of engaging and beautiful presence, and some appearance (though not at that date very marked) of delicate constitution ; of amiable refined manners, and of mild, though certainly very self-resolved, tone in conversation. I had hoped to see a good deal of him, but his early departure from

London—to which, so far as I am aware, he never returned—prevented this. He soon afterwards sent to me the MS. of his *Tiberius*, which I read, and returned to him with some observations.

Having now, since Mr. Adams's death, been invited to write a few words by way of introduction to the *Tiberius*, I readily assent. I am informed by Mr. J. W. Longsdon, the intimate friend to whom Mr. Adams confided the MS. of this play, that the author "quite recognised that, in order to ensure acceptance, Mr. Longsdon might be obliged to make considerable alterations." The same power has now been entrusted to me, and I have used it so far as I conceived to be really requisite. This I do with the less hesitation because I am also informed that in 1889, when there had been some idea of asking me to attend to an English edition of the *Songs of the Army of the Night*, Mr. Adams, writing to Mr. Longsdon and mentioning my name, said, "I would trust implicitly to his judgment in any repressions." However, that edition came out without my exercising any leading control over it, whether by means of " repressions " or otherwise.

I am not closely acquainted with the details of Adams's career, but I know that he saw much in many countries; felt much and intensely; suffered (even if we leave out of count his chronic and tormenting ill-health) much and intensely. The *Songs of the Army of the Night* are the record of his extreme opinions —which might with equal truth be called his extreme sentiments—in social, political, and religious matters; and, whatever may be the deduction which we make from them on the ground of over-vehemence in the estimate of things, and tameless fury of utterance, they are a momentous record, and will be increasingly recognised as such. They touch us too nearly at the present day to be regarded with either dispassionate calmness or indulgent allowance, but their time will assuredly come, and must in some quarters have come already. No doubt fierce sympathy and the response of hungry and shattered or outlawed hearts has greeted them

here and there; and, looking along the perspective of years, the *Songs* will be found to
have dwarfed many of the pleasant proprieties
and well-accepted sleeknesses of our days and
hours.

The deliberately planned and executed drama
of *Tiberius* is, of course, a very different sort of
production from the rapid outpouring of lyrical
rage, the clench of fierce hand to hand, the cry
of flaming spirit to spirit, which we discern in
the *Songs of the Army of the Night;* and yet
the essential and innermost core of it is by no
means unrelated to these. The same abhorrence
of dull oppression, of stolid self-indulgence
sanctioned by usage, of egotistic self-applause
drowning the call of human fellowship, speaks
out as loudly in the antique drama as in the
contemporary lyrics. But it is not on the man
and emperor Tiberius that Adams, who might
herein have followed the lead of Tacitus and
many other historians, fastens these anti-social
offences; he fastens them, on the contrary, on
the Roman aristocracy, and regards Tiberius as
the destined and conscious avenger of the mis-

deeds. Tiberius, according to his dramatist, accepts power and administers government with the express purpose of rooting out the tyrant aristocrats in the interest of the suffering populations, and is so far a public benefactor, though a ruthless sovereign. He labours to effect from above an upheaval of social forces, such as the "Army of the Night" are now, as by a clarion-cry, incited to battle for from below. That the general drift of recent historical investigation has been to take a much less dark and indignant view of the character of Tiberius than of old is a fact sufficiently well known. I am not aware, however, that Adams had been forestalled in the precise point of view which he adopts—that of a rooted hatred of Tiberius against the magnates, based on a strong sense of their public and private wickedness, and of the danger hence arising to the state, and the damage inflicted on those classes most needing imperial protection. Tiberius is generally admitted to be one of the most problematic characters in history—to some of us, one of the most fascinating. He comes down to us from Tacitus, a colossal figure of a truly portentous kind ; either portrayed accurately, or, if this is not the case, then created magnificently. Suetonius, in his inferior but still very vivid and emphatic way, tells the same tale. Not only, however, in the interest of truth and equity, but as an exercise of independent intellectual perception, it is perfectly open to any thinking man at the present day to part company with Tacitus and Suetonius, and to set forth to us a very different sort of Tiberius. Adams has done this, and I for one feel grateful to him for the enterprising spirit in which he has worked.

I have endeavoured to learn what may have been the sources from which Mr. Adams derived his conception of Tiberius, but in this I have not succeeded. Mr. Longsdon, whom I consulted, informs me that the conception had certainly been already formed before 1884, though the play had probably not by that time been written, nor perhaps even begun. The proem-verses refer to "seven long years" preceding New Year 1889 ; thus amply con-

firming, or even going beyond, Mr. Longsdon's estimate. "Adams," says this gentleman,
"never cared to talk of a thing he was writing
or going to write. He said the story, once told
even in conversation, lost its interest to him,
and he wrote afterwards with less vigour. He
was a classical man, with a leaning to scholar-
ship, and an exceedingly patient and careful
student." He regarded this drama as his best
work from a literary point of view, and in his
later days he only cared about this and the
Songs of the Army of the Night, and thought
they would live. He looked upon the *Tiberius*
as a play not unsuited for the stage, and was
fain to think that the principal personage would
be well adapted for Mr. Irving—and indeed I
am not sure but that he had in some way or
other brought the matter under the consideration of that distinguished tragedian. That Mr.
Irving might make a great deal out of the
rôle of Tiberius is clear enough; but in other
respects Mr. Adams may have been somewhat
too sanguine in these opinions, not allowing
sufficient weight to two considerations which

. B

make *Tiberius* a very difficult play to be put on the stage,—namely, the great lapse of years which its action covers, and the large element in it of mere dialogue, apart from striking action on the boards or strong scenic situation. Not, indeed, that the play is *destitute* of scenic situation, and in dramatic situation it has some truly powerful points.   As to the lapse of time, some readers may perhaps like to be reminded that no less than forty-seven years pass between Act I. and Act V.   In Act I., the divorce of Vipsania, the date is 11 B.C., the age of Tiberius 31 ; in Act II., closing with the return from Rhodes, 1 A.D., age 43 ; in Act III., the death of Augustus, 14 A.D., age 55 ; in Act IV., the fall of Sejanus, 31 A.D., age 72 ; in Act V., the death of Tiberius, 37 A.D., age 78.   Minor references throughout the play are constantly historical, and also most of the minor personages —not, I think, that of Electra : she appears to be an invention, and one of which Adams might reasonably be proud.

I find the character of Tiberius in this play to be decidedly interesting, although as a historical portrait it is, of course, disputable in a high degree. He begins as a successful and indefatigable general returned home to domestic life ; the firmest prop of the world-wide Roman state, finding home still sweeter than command and glory. He is in the fullest sense a great public man and a virtuous private man. By order of Augustus he is summoned to abandon his dearest domestic tie, and to contract a new marriage of the most distasteful kind, for purposes of state. He ponders, and, in the public interest alone and for the greatness of Rome, he assents. He even goes beyond the conception of Rome at her grandest : he hopes to aid in " the last creation, Man." We find him next degraded by an intolerable union to an intolerable woman, incapable for the present of further struggle, throwing up all public life and retiring to Rhodes, yet still resolved to be the true servant of the Roman world when the time shall come. In Rhodes he lives the life of a retired, much-cogitating philosopher, still hankering after some joy in domestic life and love. In the dialogue here between Tiberius and the

soothsayer Thrasyllus there is something which
reminds us in a remote way—certainly without
the faintest touch of imitation—of the dialogue
between Paracelsus and Aprile, in Browning's
drama of *Paracelsus*. Attaining to empire,
Tiberius devotes himself to the public weal by
general beneficence, mingled with a purpose of
quenchless severity to the " insolence of office,"
the luxurious and oppressive magnates. Con-
fiding his policy to his minister Sejanus for
practical development, he is betrayed by his
ambitious subordinate, whom at last he unmasks
and delivers over to condign punishment.
Finally, in extreme old age, everything palls
upon him—power, the exercise of will, the
rule of right, the standard of justice, the lifetime's work—and, in combating tyranny, he has
himself become a tyrant, reckless of the means,
if still not unconscious of a purpose tenaciously
conceived, unflinchingly upheld.

Mr. Adams's vindication of Tiberius proceeds
in the main (as I have already suggested) on
grounds different from those of others. The
apologists generally have aimed at showing that,

upon close and well-advised investigation, the severities of the emperor were by no means so numerous or so rigid as the reader of Tacitus is led to suppose. Adams works on a different principle. He says substantially : "Tiberius *was* severe, and he meant to be severe : but why? For the necessary and laudable purpose of extirpating a 'generation of vipers.'"

Most of the secondary characters are also imagined with vigour and presented with skill : but among these I could hardly include Sejanus, who appears to be the weakest personage in the drama ; the tangled web of treachery and criminality being woven by the greed of power upon a character which appears to be originally sentimental, impressible, and well-meaning, rather than anything else. Chærea is an arch-traitor of a still more offensive sort, but consistent enough in his meanness. Augustus is a sufficiently imposing figure ; Thrasyllus and Artaxerxes well-sustained ; Caligula (which may or may not be historically correct) a buffoon and a craven, with a touch of penetration, and full of

all wicked machinations. Julia is delineated with
extreme force, not stopping short at coarseness ;
and the winsome Greek slave-girl Electra, who
runs to seed as a cynical and wilful voluptuary,
is invented with steady insight and firm literary
and poetic touch. I must spare a word also to
the proem-lines written by Adams in Australia,
in a sort of dithyrambic prose-verse : they seem
to me super-excellent of their kind, unsurpassed
by anything of the same class.

The mention of Caligula tempts me to make
a momentary digression, for the purpose of
calling attention to a very noble drama in
which that emperor is the principal figure
—I mean *The Sentence*, by Mrs. Augusta
Webster, published some few years ago by
T. Fisher Unwin. This tragedy does not seem
to have excited so much notice as might
have been expected, but may perhaps some
day be recognised as about the *greatest* single
performance of any British poetess. Mrs.
Webster views Caligula from a standpoint quite
different from that of Adams : in fact, she con-
templates her youthful emperor with something

of the same mournful and heart-stirred sympathy with which Adams regards his elderly and aged emperor. Caligula, in *The Sentence*, is animated by a boundless passion for doing the right—he would be an embodied earthly Providence ; but the seeds of madness are in him, and he strikes tremendous and terrific blows in dusk and dark. The action of the tragedy is (unlike Adams's) concentrated and tight-knit, and the work might be capable of making a very great impression on the stage, were our time less fatally alienated than it is from the poetic drama.

In *Tiberius* the weakest act, in point of writing, seems to be the fourth, occupied with the conspiracy of Sejanus, and its discovery and punishment. Yet, as regards scenic situation, this is the strongest of all, and the most suitable for acting purposes. It may deserve remark that, in the original draft of the drama, the " Secretary in White," who takes a leading part in exhibiting the details of the conspiracy, was Tiberius himself in a temporary disguise, which at the right moment he throws off. This was certainly an incident of some dramatic force and opportunity; but Adams must have felt that it verged overmuch on melodrama, and he altered the scene into its present more sober form. I need hardly point out that Adams's version of the fall of Sejanus is not, in detail, historically true. Some incidents, such as that of Macro suddenly superseding Sejanus as commander of the Prætorian Guards, are accurate; but all about Tiberius appearing personally on the scene is a playwright's fiction—perhaps a permissible one. Yet the real fact was not a jot less dramatic: Sejanus presenting himself in the Senate in full confidence of ever-increasing honours, greeted with cringeing adulation, denounced for arrest by the written order of Tiberius, then at once hooted and execrated, and hurried off to summary execution.

The alterations which I have thought it permissible to make in this play are really few; something like eighty lines have been retrenched. They belong chiefly to the parts of Julia and Sejanus. In Adams's text some of Julia's utterances seemed so excessively violent and disagreeable as to be well omitted: the reader will not, I fancy, opine that what she is still allowed to say is at all below the due mark of unsavouriness. Sejanus had been made to indulge in a lengthy passage of sentiment regarding his deceased wife : its essence still remains, curtailed in dimension. Caligula, it will be perceived, indulges in some puns, far from being of the best : I have cut out one or two others. Apart from this matter of retrench-ment, I have applied myself, here and there, to keeping the verses more accurate in scansion than they used to be—for this is a point as to which Adams seemed to allow himself more than a profitable amount of latitude or of laxity. The reader may, however, rely upon it that the whole of what I have done is a trifle, and that the play remains, to all practical intents and purposes, the same identical play which Adams wrote. To alter it in any serious degree would have been an act of presumption on my part, and one which I must disclaim, whether in principle or in fact.

" Spoiled by power " seems to be the ruling idea in the drama of *Tiberius*. Tiberius himself is certainly spoiled to some extent, though I do not understand that Mr. Adams intended, even in the final act, to represent him as bereft of some sense of public duty and justifiable policy. He dies with the words "Rome, Rome!" upon his lips. Augustus is in fuller degree exempted from the ban : the author of the *Songs of the Army of the Night* was not likely to regard his imperium with entire sympathy, but nothing in the play indicates disapproval of its general scope and aim. Julia is spoiled by power in one way ; Caligula, by the hope or expectation of power, in another ; Sejanus and Electra, not to speak of Chærea and Macro, each in their several ways. This is one of the lessons stamped on the front of imperial Rome, and from of old legible to all men.

"Spoiled by power." It is an awful doom, and an awful subject for tragic drama. Adams has treated it with breadth and force, with deep human sympathy, with due dignity and unstinted realism, and with a large measure of poetic strength and handling. There is brain in his purpose and life-blood in his work, and the noble army of dramatists may, in virtue of this posthumous tragedy, enrol him in their ranks.

W. M. ROSSETTI.

LONDON, *March* 1894.

TIBERIUS.

DRAMATIS PERSONÆ.

AUGUSTUS	
SCRIBONIA	*His divorced wife.*
JULIA I.	*Their daughter.*
GAIUS CÆSAR	
LUCIUS CÆSAR	
JULIA II.	*Julia's children.*
AGRIPPINA	
AGRIPPA	
POSTUMUS	
LIVIA	*Wife of Augustus and mother of Tiberius and Drusus I. by a former marriage.*
TIBERIUS	
VIPSANIA	*His wife.*
DRUSUS II.	*Their son.*
DRUSUS I.	*Brother to Tiberius.*
ANTONIA	*His wife.*
GERMANICUS	*Their children.*
LIVILLA	
CALIGULA	*Son of Germanicus and Agrippina.*
SEJANUS	*Minister of Tiberius.*
AELIA	*His daughter.*
CHÆREA	*Officers in the Pretorian Guards.*
MACRO	
THRASYLLUS	*A soothsayer.*
ARTAXERXES	*A eunuch, attendant on Tiberius.*
MATHO	*A coppersmith.*
ELECTRA	*A Greek slave.*
A SECRETARY.	

PRIESTS, PRIESTESSES, SOLDIERS, SLAVES, PEOPLE.

ACT I.

Rome. A room in TIBERIUS' *house. Morning.*

VIPSANIA (*at the window*).

Tiberius ! . . . husband ! . . . husband !

[*Enter* TIBERIUS.

TIBERIUS.

Didst thou call ?

Well, what is there to see ?

VIPSANIA (*in his arm*).

First there is . . .

TIBERIUS.

Thou ?

VIPSANIA.

Yes, I. Is that enough, or want'st thou more ?

TIBERIUS.

Enough, and more—more than enough, sweet
    wife !

VIPSANIA.

But wilt thou say so when I tell thee what
I saw right up the street ? I think thou lov'st
    him

More than thou lov'st me, or my Drusus either,
Thy Drusus? No? Thou dost not love thy
    brother
More than myself who sat and spun at home
While you two won such glory at the wars?
I am not all of ice, as his wife is,
Lady Antonia, nor is Drusus (mine)
Like her Germanicus, but we both think
Livilla is more like my child than hers—
She has such pretty curls and such white
    skin ! . . .
And now I'll say, since thou behav'st so well,
Just how I felt when Drusus came with thee
Out of the hall to find me yesterday.
Well, I felt jealous, and that is the truth !
You never put your arm round me like that !

          TIBERIUS.
Never ?

          VIPSANIA.
    No, wicked, never !—never before. . . .
                  [*He kisses her.*
          TIBERIUS.
It may be, dear, that all lies in that word,
That one short word " before." Now I look
    back,

And think on our past life, and all I did,
And all I did not, that might make it happy
For thee, I seem a sinner, and I ask
Humbly forgiveness. It is ill, I know,
To have been so strange to thee so long. I
    dreamed :
I did thee wrong in dreaming. Never think
That I was cold with a deliberate aim.
I was not, thou believ'st it ? All my youth
(If ever I was young) was with my masters,
My books, and the great statecraft that they kept
(As great Augustus bade them) for my portion.
If I had any love, or knew of it,
It was for him, my brother, this brave Drusus,
The hero and the glory of our house !
We married. Thou wert patient, quiet, sweet :
So quiet and so patient that thy sweetness,
Sweet wife, grew round me unobserved, as vines
Twine round the elms, and the green garland-
    leaves
Bore vintage of the purple fruit of love,
Ere I awakened. This, my gentle home
With thee and with our boy, clasped me all
    round,

Until the sap-blood of the two ran one.
And yet I never knew it till I lost it.

VIPSANIA.

That is very pretty, just like poetry !
But they are coming ; they're gone in now—

Drusus,

Antonia and Livilla and Germanicus.

TIBERIUS.

Was I blind and deaf, with senses all awry ?
Not quite, since I awakened there at last.
Slowly I grew to see
How well I loved thee and the lad and here,
Our home with all it held.   Thou'lt surely smile
If I should tell thee how, for long, I dared not
To speak of this to Drusus, and at last
Broke to him, and for hours at nights we two
Would sit and talk of our loved ones in Rome,
The happiest hours of those devouring days
When victory crowned us ! . . .

VIPSANIA.

Hush, here they come ! No, let me go, Tiberius !
I am all tumbled and my hair put out !

TIBERIUS.

Kiss me again, then !

VIPSANIA.

O now let me go !

[*He kisses her.*

I am quite ashamed !

[*Enter* DRUSUS I., ANTONIA, GERMANICUS
and LIVILLA.

Welcome, lady Antonia and good brother.

TIBERIUS.

Why, kiss her, Drusus ! Perhaps she'll kiss thee
    better
Than she will me.

VIPSANIA.

Tiberius ! What a husband !
Antonia is not plagued so !

[*Enter* DRUSUS II.

Well, dear children !
Here comes cousin Drusus at the very moment !

TIBERIUS (*to* DRUSUS I.).

Look at the lads.

DRUSUS I.

Livilla must be kissed,
Or there'll be crying for it.

VIPSANIA (*to* DRUSUS II.).

Kiss her, Drusus.
Antonia, will you come within ?

DRUSUS I.

       Augustus
Is close behind us with Livia and Julia.

   GERMANICUS (*to* DRUSUS II.).
Dost thou kiss girls ?

    DRUSUS II.

    Why, yes, if they are pretty.

    GERMANICUS.
Didst thou go to the shows ?

    DRUSUS II.

       I went outside,
But father would not let me see the fights.
Didst *thou* go ?

    GERMANICUS.

   No. My father does not wish it.

    LIVILLA.
Now, Drusus, wilt thou take me, please, inside,
And show me thy three birds, and play with me ?

    DRUSUS II.
Wilt thou come too, Germanicus ?

    GERMANICUS.

      Yes, I come.
[GERMANICUS, DRUSUS II., *and* LIVILLA *go out.*

VIPSANIA.

Why are the men both laughing so ?   Tiberius,
Augustus with thy mother and with Julia
And her two sons, Antonia says, are come
To visit us, and are only just behind.

TIBERIUS.

So Drusus tells me.

VIPSANIA.

What was't made thee laugh so ?

TIBERIUS.

The children.   Didst thou hear Livilla there ?—
" Now, Drusus, wilt thou take me, please, inside,
And show me thy three birds, and play with
	me."
And straight he takes her hand and leads her in,
Germanicus following like a Greek tragedian.

VIPSANIA.

She's a sweet child !

ANTONIA.

I fear a forward child,
That soon knows those who love her overwell,
And asks the most of them.

VIPSANIA.

Hush, here they are !

[*Enter* Augustus, Livia, Julia I., Gaius
     and Lucius Cæsar.

Welcome, sire.

         Augustus.

         Ah, you, Tiberius ?

         Tiberius.

                 Welcome, sire.

Welcome, dear mother.

         Augustus.

         Julia.

         Julia.

             Yes, father.

         Vipsania (*to* Antonia).

What beautiful, bold boys !

         Antonia (*to* Vipsania).

           Bolder, I think,

Than beautiful, even as their mother is.

         Augustus.

Julia, this is our twin-helmed glorious Mars,
Or one of them. Ah, Drusus ? Here's the other !
The women now all run to look on you,
And we, unwarlike seniors, shut our eyes
And blink abashed like candles light-eclipsed.

LIVIA.

Thou dost belie our sex.   Although at night
We watch, perchance, some star peerless and
    bright,
By daytime there's the sun, and he alone
Can blind us.

AUGUSTUS (*to* ANTONIA).

            Would you think, lady, that we
Were an old married couple?   What a wife
To make such pretty speeches—such years after!
My dear, beware yet how thou talkest so.
Here is thy Zeno Drusus; he who holds
The Republic brooks no ruler, no sole sun
To wheel above it, lord of light and heat.
Is it not so, Cypriote?

DRUSUS.

            Sire, we take
What the great gods shall give us, and therewith
Shall strive to do our duty.

AUGUSTUS.

                    Nobly said!

And were all togaed shorn aristocrats
Like to our Drusus, Rome and Italy
Were Saturn's land again.

LIVIA (*to* VIPSANIA).
                    Take us within.
                    [LIVIA *and* VIPSANIA *go out.*

JULIA (*to* ANTONIA).
Indeed I think this heat and dust are frightful.
I hate the city.   We shall go to Baiæ
To-morrow.   When do you go to the country?

ANTONIA.
Not yet awhile, my lady Julia.
My husband has affairs here with his clients,
And other matters.

JULIA.
                    Oh !—Excuse me yawning.
I'm yawning dreadfully to-day—quite sleepy.

ANTONIA.
They have gone in.

JULIA.
                    Have they ?   Gaius and Lucius,
Come in with us.

ANTONIA (*to* DRUSUS I.).
Come, they would be alone.   The Emperor
Would speak with him.

                    [ANTONIA *and* DRUSUS I. *go out.*

JULIA (*at the curtains*).

        Well, my Gaius ?   Well,
My Lucius ?   What say ye to this fine house ?

GAIUS.

They are all fools here.

LUCIUS.

        A poor sort of place.
I think it's rather fusty.

JULIA (*laughing*).

        Oh, you rude boys !
" Not yet awhile, my lady Jul—i—a ! " (*going*)

      [JULIA I., GAIUS *and* LUCIUS *go out.*

AUGUSTUS.

Tiberius.

TIBERIUS.

    Sire.

AUGUSTUS.

        I think you know I—love you :
Yea, I'll say love ; for hope and trust's affection
Mount to the word the amorous women use.
Indeed I let you see so, six years gone,
In Gaul with me, and I, I do not change. . . .
I like your silence, yet I'd bid you tell me
You do believe this.

TIBERIUS.

        That I am trusted, sire,
I knew, and that you hold me kindly, I knew,
And I was glad and proud.

             AUGUSTUS.

                  There, there, that's well !
We leave these things, save as they touch our
    state.
Tiberius, I have but one child.   Your mother,
The partner of some cares, the soother of all,
Is childless : this hath been so.   Tell me, friend,
What think you of the lads ?

             TIBERIUS.

                   They're noble lads.

             AUGUSTUS.

Gaius and Lucius, noble lads, you say ?
And your own boy, and Drusus' boy and girl—
We are well found in young.   If I were gone,
The man to rear and mould those noble lads
Is he I have such hope and trust of.

             TIBERIUS.

                    I ?

            AUGUSTUS.

You.   Yea, and how all this bears final fruit

Is this—that, if they grow not as they should
Who follow in such tracks as Julius threw,
And (I will say) such as Augustus leaves,—
Or, if they die,—who is it that should hold
The helm of the great world-ship but Tibe-
    rius? . . .
I praise your silence still.   There is no need
Of words before the face of what's to do
Other than yea or nay.   I think I know
That, were the hour of such a choice to come
As lay betwixt the unworthiness of sons
And worthiness of one who is but a friend,
Tiberius would not fail us.   Ponder this,
All its full meaning, at another time.
Break speech now to say yea.   For there is more.
Speak.

TIBERIUS.

      I am silent, not before your words,
Sire, and the heavy charge you'd lay on me :
Not, I would say, because I cannot see
What is their meaning, even to the full,
But . . .

AUGUSTUS.

    Speak again.   Augustus bids you speak.

TIBERIUS.

It is too great a charge for me, too high,
Too far above the haunts of kindly men
Among the peaks of pure and parching light.
I felt it as we stood there that fair morn
On the Dalmatian hills, Drusus and I,
Cold though the sun was blazing, clear though
    all
The camp lay swathed in mist.　Sire, I will take
The guardian's place to Gaius and to Lucius,
If they should ever need it.　I trust not.
My father with brave Lucius and fierce Fulvia,—
My father cleaved to your great foe Antonius,
Yet was he proud to give his sons to you,
And they you know forget not how that pride
Found gratitude and glory in your actions.
Our hands and heads and hearts are yours for
    ever !

AUGUSTUS.

So be it.　But, look you, they're but lads, and
    lads
That have a mother that was surely changed
At birth or in her cradle with Antonia.
Antonia is my daughter ; Julia his.

How from the fond fool that Scribonia was
Came forth this pantheress?
Three days ago I saw Mæcenas. Well,
'Twas pity that it went so 'twixt us twain,
For he is passing from us, wise Mæcenas!
I've spoken with him. Both our minds are one.
There is a single foot can follow on
Where we have followed Julius. It may be
That Gaius (he's the better of the two)
Shall take his shape as you shall mould. If not,
Why, he must go! I leave all that to him
Whom I now call my son, my. grandsons'
    father. . . .
Look not so strangely. We will try all things
To make our Gaius worthy. The first need
For such a trial is the tamer. .You
Shall tame our pantheress. . . . Do you under-
    stand?
You look but strangely.

TIBERIUS.

            Tame her? Marry her? . . .
Vipsania. . . .

AUGUSTUS.

            Hah, Vipsania? It cannot be
You hold by her?

TIBERIUS.

Stop, stop, you kill me, sire!

AUGUSTUS.

I cannot think this is Tiberius here
That reels and stammers.

TIBERIUS.

No, I cannot do it!
She, Julia, Julia, she?   No, never, never! . . .
Sire, let me speak.   I could not shame myself
To be the scoff of Rome.

AUGUSTUS.

Who speaks of scoffs?
I say she shall be tamed, with iron rods
If she will have it so, with rods red-hot.
I've told her, and she knows it too, she knows it!
I'll brook no more.

TIBERIUS.

Vipsania—

AUGUSTUS.

Do not give me
That foolish name! You've learned my purpose.
    Here—
Here is your mother.

                            [*Re-enter* LIVIA.

LIVIA.

My son !   Tiberius !

TIBERIUS.

Mother ?

LIVIA.

What troubles you ?   It is too much,
Too great a burthen for its suddenness ?
I judged our own Tiberius braver, stronger
Than such a face as this.

AUGUSTUS (*with a gesture to* LIVIA).

We go within.

[*He goes out.*

LIVIA.

This is the greatest day of both our lives.
Look up !   Thou tremblest ?   Nay, I say, look
   up !
The Empress wills it. . . . Ah, my son, forgive
   me !
I had not spoken so but for thy face
That seemed a palsied madman's.   Stare not so :
Thou almost frightenest me.   The whole wide
   world
Lies at our feet to take it up and pluck it
And wield as a sceptre.

TIBERIUS.

Mother . . .

LIVIA.

Well ?

Speak ; I will listen, listen and—obey.

TIBERIUS.

Follow him.   Leave me here alone awhile :
Then come, and I will tell thee what I'll do.
I'll tell thee by a sign.   Bring them all in,
And let Augustus know—let only him.
If I shall come and speak to Julia,
And take her hand, and say good-day to her—
(For they must go, you all must go on this :
Tell Drusus and Antonia), then . . . then . . .

LIVIA.

Yes ?

TIBERIUS.

I'll do it.   But, if to Vipsania
And take *her* hand, be sure not all the earth
Shall stay me from *my* purpose—to be—gone !

LIVIA.

Begone ?   Where wouldst thou go ?

TIBERIUS (*with a gesture*).

I . . . Woman, woman,

That will suffice.   Go in and leave me now.

[LIVIA goes out.

O, here before mine eyes Fate's Gordian knot,
And her Sphinx-beast behind it, ravenous,
Breathes on my face.   To think—to make my
    thought
The sword to cut what I may not unravel,
How can I, who yet must ?   Life, life and
    time, . . .
O youth, O dreams that end in this mad hour !
All the great past arrays itself like ghosts
Of two death-armies grappling to the fray
That earth has yet to see.   Here, here alone,
Utterly naked and forlorn of all,
A pigmy in the clash of terrible powers
That raise him to the cheek of the great sun
Or whelm him in the ocean-depths, I stand
And make my choice. Once chosen, 'tis for ever !
I, who am I that I should spurn content ?
I, what am I that I should choose renown ?
To me what glory outshines happiness ? ·
To me what life's reward compares with that
Of the great deed done and the world made free ?
Perchance that happiness may sour and sear ?

D

Perchance that deed in doing may be marred ?
There is no chance of both, with joy of both
And grief of both, but grief and joy of one. . . .
Sever, O clouds !   Rise up, and let the sun
Break in on me.   Give me more air and light !
I see a hundred puny men rise up,
And babbling voices, eyes that cannot guess
The huge perspective Julius gazes on,
Hands weaker than the seas and lands he held
A cup within his palms and brooded o'er.
Then, look, Augustus comes, and from the mists
Clears it here, there, there, here, and sheds à
      beam
Of mild and equal radiance over all.
Romans rise up wherever Roman blood
Has bred the seed of soldier-citizens.
A nation's lost ; a race is merged in what
Is Empire and the last creation—*Man !*
The peace, the great peace, laps a world as great,
And over it, raising all men to be
Men, more than Romans, look, the Emperor !
Gods that are men, this is a deed so great
That but to spend the heart, the soul, the mind
In its attempt lifts up a man to God !

And I am bidden take it, humbly, bravely,
I, even I. I take it ! I renounce
All that shall stand between that deed and me !

[*Re-enter* AUGUSTUS, LIVIA, JULIA, GAIUS,
    LUCIUS, DRUSUS I., ANTONIA, VIPSANIA,
    DRUSUS II., GERMANICUS *and* LIVILLA.
    TIBERIUS *goes slowly towards* JULIA.

LIVIA.

And, as thou say'st, my Julia, these garments
Are fitter for the winter than such heat
As this last month's has been.   But ah, I fear
Our Roman women dress too richly now ;
Extravagance is but immodesty
In peacock covering.   The old times were best.

JULIA I.

O, it's the horrid colours that they wear—
The sight of their great piles of purple blankets
Strapped on to them like packages on mules.
Did Cleopatra ever dress like that ?

LIVIA.

Dear child, thou must not speak this way to us.
It shocks us.   We are simple Roman ladies.

JULIA I.

O, Cleopatra ?   That is true.   She shocked

Your father, Antonia.   So they say, at least.

GAIUS.

Marcus Antonius was like Alexander.

He was a soldier.   I shall be like him,

And I shall conquer Persia.

JULIA I.

Then, young cockerel,

Thou must take heed of shocking Cleopatras.

LUCIUS.

What will they do ?   A woman can't do much.

GAIUS.

I'm not afraid of women shocking *me !*

TIBERIUS.

Lady, fair Julia, a happy day !

[*He takes her hand.*

JULIA I.

Why, the man gave me quite a fright !   Good-
day.

His hand's like clammy steel.   Good-day, then,
ladies.

VIPSANIA.

Good-day, lady.

[JULIA, GAIUS *and* LUCIUS *go out.*

LIVIA (*to* TIBERIUS).

That was well done, my son.

AUGUSTUS (*to* DRUSUS I.).

Well, you will come, then, soon ? (to-morrow
    morning,
If it will suit), and we will talk of it.
Come to the supper : come whene'er you please ;
You're heartily welcome always.

DRUSUS I.

I thank you, sire. I will not fail to see you
To-morrow morning.

        [AUGUSTUS *and* LIVIA *go out.*

VIPSANIA.

        Well, the Emperor
Was very pleasant, I think ; he paid me such—
Such pretty compliments !—and thee too,
    Antonia.
He can be very gracious when he wishes,
Like all the men !

ANTONIA.

        He has, in desperate days
Of ruin and revenge, alone been nobly
Moderate and great, and so we honour him.

DRUSUS I.

My wife, thou speakest as my very soul !

LIVILLA.

I do not like Gaius and Lucius, nor
Does Drusus, nor Germanicus.   We think
They are very rude.   They never spoke to us.

TIBERIUS.

Gaius and Lucius never spoke to thee?

VIPSANIA.

My dear, thou hast frighted her with thy wild
    laugh !
O, poor Livilla !   There, there, do not cry !
Kiss me.

TIBERIUS.

    Our weakness is our worst contempt.

ANTONIA (*to* DRUSUS I.).

What ails Tiberius ?

DRUSUS I.

        I cannot tell thee.
But in the room my mother whispered me
That we should follow them at once away.
I think Augustus spoke to him some matter
Of anxious moment.   Take the children, go.

ANTONIA (*to* GERMANICUS).

Come . . . Come, Livilla.   Farewell, then, Vip-
    sania.

(*To* TIBERIUS.)

Brother, farewell.

TIBERIUS.

Farewell, sister, farewell.

DRUSUS I. (*to* TIBERIUS).

I will be with thee in the afternoon.

TIBERIUS.

Farewell. Yes, yes, in the afternoon. Farewell !

[DRUSUS I., ANTONIA, GERMANICUS, LIVILLA
and DRUSUS II. *go out.*

VIPSANIA (*at the window*).

I cannot think that Julia chose her colours
So very nicely as *she* thinks she does !
I am sure she dresses more like some freedwoman.

TIBERIUS.

Vipsania.

VIPSANIA.

Yes. . . .

TIBERIUS.

I pray thee do not fear.
Give me thy hand. I pray thee do not fear. . . .
Vipsania, at this place our pathways sever.
No man that lives can change it. We must part.

VIPSANIA.

Must part, Tiberius ?

TIBERIUS.

           That was the word.
Let then, our steps fall quickly. Simply, plainly,
Thou art my wife no more, and I no more
Thy husband. 'Tis no sin, no fault, no jot
Of aught undone or done by thee brings this.
On thee no shadow of dishonour falls.
Mistrust I never had.   I thought—I think
Vipsania patient, loving, pure and true.

VIPSANIA.

What have I done ?

TIBERIUS.

           O by the gods, I say
Nothing !   I ask, I do beseech of thee
To hold it in this way.   Fate is too strong.
Listen.   I am the Emperor's elect
To mould and guide his grandsons to his place.
And, should they die,
I, I am he who must fulfil the deeds
Of Julius and Augustus.   For this end
He wills—Fate wills—Rome and the whole
    world will
I marry Julia.

VIPSANIA.

Marry Julia ? Julia ?

Oh, oh !

TIBERIUS.

Thou shudderest at it ? Why, I say
It is not I who marry her—Tiberius
That marries Julia. Were that so, just so,
I'd kill her. O Vipsania, we who live
Here on this peak, where power's sunrise and
  set
Flash on us last and first, while down below,
From out the shadow and the spreading light,
The people hold us gods,—an icy air
Of cold compulsion leads us on our lives,
Play-actors, puppets of our parts ordained
From long ago. And though it rive our hearts,
Thus must we speak, thus much, no more, no less,
Or face the hisses that the coward wins
From those his soul despises.

DRUSUS II. (*within*).

Mother, mother !

VIPSANIA.

Drusus, my Drusus !

TIBERIUS (*approaching her*).

    Stay ;—stay, and remember.
Think you. Your father was Agrippa, he
Who swayed the Actium storm of war : who gave
The wife he loved, to take Marcellus' place
And raise up to Augustus very seed
Of that divinest stock which thrones the world :
Yea, and (the fitting crown of this and him)
Who held the seeming death-struck Emperor's
  ring,
Elect to that great task that is a god's !

    DRUSUS II. (*within*).

Mother !

     [*Re-enter* DRUSUS II.

    VIPSANIA.

Julia, my father's wife, and now my husband's—

    TIBERIUS.

Remember . . . Well, my boy, why stand'st
  thou thus
Looking from her to me, from me to her ?
  (*Seated.*)
Come to thy father. Drusus, that is thy mother.
She's leaving us, for she must go away.

DRUSUS II.

Why must she leave us, father? Where's she
    going?
Where art thou going, mother?

TIBERIUS.

Look at me, Drusus,
Right in the eyes. Thy mother leaves us now,
This very hour, and will not say good-bye,
Because we must be brave, we must be Romans.

DRUSUS II.

But is it Roman not to say good-bye?

TIBERIUS (*with a gesture to* VIPSANIA).

Ay, very Roman—of the modern stamp (*hold-
ing* DRUSUS II.'s *head in his hands*).
My lad, I think thou'lt be a brave lad always,
Not like thy father, who's a sorry coward.

               [VIPSANIA *goes out.*

DRUSUS II.

Why, thou art crying, father? Why, thine eyes
Are full of tears.

TIBERIUS.

Tears? No, Drusus, but rheum.
But think, boy, of the amphitheatre,
How in the arena men sword it to death,

Or the Pursuer sees the trident up
To stab him through the meshes.   Thou must go
And see the shows on the ides.   Both of us
Will go with the Emperor.

DRUSUS II.

O that's grand, that's grand !
And shall I see them fight ?

TIBERIUS.

Ay, ay.

DRUSUS II.

And shall I
Put down my thumb as all the street-men do ?

TIBERIUS.

Or turn it up, if he have foughten well.

DRUSUS II.

Yes, if he's foughten well : but not, if not.
But mine aunt Julia always turns hers down ;
I heard her say so.   Where is mother gone ?

TIBERIUS.

Thy mother's gone away.   Thy mother now
Is Julia.   Gaius and Lucius are thy brothers.

DRUSUS II.

Father, I'd go to mother now, I think,
But thou art paining so.

TIBERIUS.
>   To Julia ?   Mother ?
I am ashamed.   Our breed has lost its bones.
Go to her, Drusus, go and say good-bye.

DRUSUS II.
And shall I say good-bye for thee, too, father ?
I'd say it like a Roman.   Shall I, father ?

TIBERIUS.
For me too, for me too.

DRUSUS II.
>   Thou art very sad (*going*).
But I will show thee how my new top goes
When I come back.   (*Returns.*)   So kiss me,
>   father dear.
>   TIBERIUS (DRUSUS II. *going*).
Go, go thou also.   [DRUSUS II. *goes out.*
>   I must be alone.
Alone through all the years till weary death
Closes these heavy lids, and I can sleep,
And wake no more.   Now, courage, courage !
>   pride,
I never called thee yet who call thee now.
Farewell, the love of woman !   Farewell, all

The sweet sure peace wherein dwelt heavenly
    faith.
Farewell, dear home and gentle sanctities
And pure content, and heart—and soul—loosed
    speech,
And that true self I nevermore shall know !——
Alone, alone, for ever and ever alone !

ACT II.

SCENE I.

Rome. A room in TIBERIUS' *new house. After-noon.* SCRIBONIA, JULIA I., JULIA II., AGRIPPINA, *and* POSTUMUS.

SCRIBONIA.

Julia.

JULIA I.

Well, what ?

SCRIBONIA.

Thou art sad to-day, my child.
What ails thee ?

JULIA I.

Ails me ?   Ailing, I suppose,
Or this wet weather.   It should rain at nights.

SCRIBONIA.

Why dost thou gaze so at the children there ?

JULIA I.

There are two more.   I reckon up the pain
These five have cost me, and not one of them

A jot of pleasure since.   They should not live.
In Carthage they had sacrifices of them.

SCRIBONIA.

My child, and yet I loved thee, and I love.

JULIA I.

I cannot tell you why.   You ne'er desired me,—
And ached to bruise your lips with kissing mine.
I never gave you aught.   I never loved you.
My father never loved you.   O these dull days!
He's a poor fool.

SCRIBONIA.

My child thou dost not know him.

JULIA I.

" My child, my child ? "   Well, Julia, who's thy
  father ?

SCRIBONIA.

Hush, hush, dear : let the children be.

JULIA I.

And Drusus,
Where's Drusus ?   He must tell us who's his
  father . . .
Who is *my* father ?   No, I'll not believe
That grey old snake's my father—not Augustus—

[Repulses JULIA II.

AGRIPPINA.
      Mother is ill to-day.
JULIA. II.
I hate her, I hate her.
AGRIPPINA.
        She is our mother,
And we should love her.
JULIA II.
        When I am a woman,
I'll tell her that I always hated her.
She never gives me sweets or anything.
POSTUMUS.
Sister, what doth thou thay?
JULIA II.
        What do I *thay?*
But if thou listen to us, I will pinch thee
Up in the room. . . .
JULIA I.
       I wonder why I talk?
I am quite weary of you. I have known you
So many years.
SCRIBONIA.
      Yea, I it was that bore thee ;
Nourished thee at these breasts : for day and night

E

Wept when they took thee from me : blessed
  them then
When I might see and hold thee : straight
  forgot
All my great wrongs, when of his clemency
Thy father would permit me to be with thee.

JULIA I.

It is your folly.   Women all have such.
There is no use in motherhood, *I* think.

SCRIBONIA.

To Scipio also did I bear two children,
And loved them ; yea, but not as I loved thee.

JULIA I.

He's a poor fool, too, this Tiberius,
My husband !
Could he not be the greatest man in Rome ?
Agrippa never was so great as he ;
For now he both has the " tribunal power "
And is called Imperator.   And yet when
My father's dead, this pedagogue-in-chief
Will rear my whelps up to the rulership !
Why could he not rule as the Prince himself ?
These Neros, only fit for school-masters !

SCRIBONIA.

Nero is " brave," and at Metaurus stream
Rome knew the name was equal to the men.

JULIA I.

No ; Drusus would not have me. Why ?
  " Because—.
Because he loved and honoured " that white block,
His wife, and that black-browed blockhead, his
    brother,
My husband !

SCRIBONIA.

    O no, no ! Thou ne'er did'st that.

JULIA I.

And now he's dead, and my Tiberius blubbered,
Or would have blubbered, but I was by to see.
He loved that mincing, heifer wife of his.
He had a pretty smile when I informed him
She'd married Gallus. Gallus ! Any one
Who had a house for babies and the rest
Could marry her !

SCRIBONIA.

    Antonia loved her husband,
One of two peerless brothers, fellows in arms,
Rome's Dioscuri, and Vipsania did.

And were it so with thee, my wayward child,
Thou wouldst be happier.

JULIA I.

That is idle talk !
One is not happy with these politic men ;
One but endures them.   He's so great he thinks,
He'd not offend his cast-off shoes.   He apes
Julius,—yes, he, with his big goggle eyes
That see, like a cat's, in the dark.   Why, Julius,
He was a man, and (or the women told lies)
He knew what kissing meant.   So, here he comes,
My politic, puling, Dioscurus husband !

[*Enter* TIBERIUS.

TIBERIUS.

Good-morrow, ladies.

SCRIBONIA.

And to thee, Tiberius.

TIBERIUS (*to* SCRIBONIA).

Take out the children.

JULIA I.

Take thyself with them,
And we'll say thanks.   Your warriorship has
   come
To play at Agamemnon, and that's stale.

TIBERIUS (*to* SCRIBONIA).

Take out the children.

SCRIBONIA.

Children, come.

JULIA II.

I won't.

AGRIPPINA.

Yes, Julia, come.

JULIA II.

I won't, I won't !   I'll bite thee, if thou touchest me.

[SCRIBONIA, AGRIPPINA, *and* POSTHUMUS
go out.

JULIA II.

I *will* stop, if I want.

TIBERIUS.

Julia, go out.

JULIA II.

Eugh, eugh !   He'll throttle me, mother.   Eugh, eugh !

TIBERIUS.

Go out.   [JULIA II. *goes out.*

JULIA I.

'Tis something fine to fright a child !

That is the way you win your triumphs, you
    know.
Go a procession with a trousered ape,
To stick him up for another trousered ape,
And come back conqueror of Armenia !
You've victories to be proud of.   You a soldier ?
A copying clerk !

TIBERIUS.

        I have a few words for you,
If you will listen to me.

JULIA I.

          I always listen ;
You're so amusing.   But do not blush and
    stammer.
It makes me think of our marriage night.

TIBERIUS.

                What—what
I have to say is very simple.   Here
I hold some letters.

JULIA I.

      Mine.   And did you steal them ?

TIBERIUS.

The man you sent them to has blazoned them
Around all Rome.

JULIA I.

    Most men do that.   Why, Gallus . . .
No hurry with your remarks.   I am just ripe
To say all sorts of pleasant things to you.
You *are* amusing.   Truly you cannot figure
How odd you look !

TIBERIUS.

        What I have come to tell you
Is this. We part forthwith. Not one more night
The same roof covers us.

        [*Enter* LIVIA *behind.*

JULIA I.

        I feel quite faint.
Will you, please, hand that phial there to me ?
No, in the niche there. Thank you. You ob-
   served ?

TIBERIUS.

I shall leave Rome at evening.   Artaxerxes
Has the full power to treat with you and make
What best arrangement pleases you.

JULIA I.

             Ah ?—Well,
I wish you a good voyage. Going again
To Germany ?

TIBERIUS.

These letters—

JULIA I.

                I suppose
They are Julius Antonius' ?   Julius always had
The wretchedest taste.

TIBERIUS.

           These letters I may use
As proof to the Emperor, should he hinder me.

JULIA I.

A slave is listening there behind the curtains.
No, it's your mother ! Please, mother, come in.
Thou'lt get those aches again in thy legs with
    the draughts.
Thou'rt very careless.

LIVIA.

Shameless and abandoned—

TIBERIUS.

Mother, be calmer. In the flinging of filth,
He does best who goes another way.
The storm is nigh the turn when at the worst.
These things are ending now.

LIVIA.

           It is Augustus !
           [*Enter* AUGUSTUS.

TIBERIUS.

Mother, thou'lt leave me to speak. . . .

AUGUSTUS.

What means this, son ?

TIBERIUS.

It's meaning, sire, is clear.   I ask your leave
For quitting Rome. My name here is the
    scarecrow
The very brothels jeer at.   It is too much ?
Never again one roof for her and me.
My plaint is not alone for common wrongs,
The mixture of my shame with the infamy
Of such as Julius, the ancient master-usher
Of a hundred rank debauches, but that she,
My wife, has fouled the very public places,
Revelling a mimic Egyptian wanton there
Before the greasy leers of the gutter slaves.

AUGUSTUS.

Julia, is this true ?

JULIA I.

Father, that man
Is a tailor, and eats leeks.   Phœbe, my woman,
Can never scent the room enough when he's gone
I have to keep the windows open wide
When he sits by me.   He sleeps in his clothes.

LIVIA.

Vicious !

JULIA I.

Who vicious ?   I, my mother, I ?
O sanctified ex-spouse. . . .

LIVIA.

Thou lollest there,
Insolent creature with thy laughing lips,
To lash me with thy foul and venomous tongue
To fury.   I could—strike thee ! . . .

TIBERIUS.

Dear mother, calm !   Let not mine own white
    words
Make thine red-hot.   Sire, all I say I know,
And, proof of it, here for your eyes to see.
I do demand you let me part from her
Now and irrevocably, at once, for ever !

AUGUSTUS.

Julia.

JULIA I.

Father ?

AUGUSTUS.

Are these things he says
True ?

Tiberius.

Sire, and would you doubt me that I lie?
Were you another man than what you are—

Livia.

Hush, my son, hush, Augustus must be just,
Even as the great gods are.

Augustus.

I asked thee, daughter,
Were these things true?

Julia I.

What things?

Augustus.

The offence, it seems,
He charges on thee is unfaithfulness
With Julius Antonius, him who is alive
And fouling Rome only because thy prayers
And promises kept him from the hangman. Answer,
Answer me.

Julia I.

He has proofs—my letters—he says.

Augustus.

This public revel? . . .

JULIA I.

My husband keeps a pack of private jackals.
His eunuch Artaxerxes, that is one,
Or the star-gazer whom he brought us back
From his Armenian triumph—Dra—, Thrasyllus,
I think his name is. Any of them will swear
All that he wants. That is their use to him.

AUGUSTUS.

Rise and go forth.

JULIA I.

Father ?

AUGUSTUS.

Rise and go forth.
I say begone.

JULIA I.

Strike me ! I'm not afraid.

AUGUSTUS.

Out, out !   [JULIA I. *goes out.*
And Livia, you too, go this way.
Leave us. Fear nothing. Go, my dear, go, go.
We shall be better. I will speak with thee
Presently. Thanks, dear.   [LIVIA *goes out.*
. . . If all these things are thus, why, my Ti-
berius,
Have left them silently corrode so long ?

That is not wise ; it ruffles calmer thoughts.
What say you—ha ?

TIBERIUS.

        I am unhinged—undone !
I can no more.   I must get hence and know
The balm of quiet nature, and purity
Of simple lives.   I pine, I hunger and thirst
For thought, for peace.   Mine eyes are dizzy and
    dim—
It is not days and weeks, not months, but years,
But years and ages that my void soul craves.
Void ?   It is dead.   My body perishes too. . . .
I stood by Drusus, by my brother's side,
And held his hand, and saw the wide world lose
    him
And all that made its emptiness seem dear.
Sire, I have striven too much and borne too
    much.
I pray you let me go—release me !

AUGUSTUS.

              Go ?
Where would you go ?

TIBERIUS.

    To Rhodes.   It is all planned.

Years past I marked the place for my repose.
Let naught be changed of what you hope of me.
What I have chosen as great, greater than life,
I choose again to-day.   But let me go,
If you would have me do it.   Let me go !
No little strip of a half-foreign sky
Where the familiar blue grows pale and stale,
Utterly vigourless with its jaded air,
But league-long draughts of strange deliciousness,
Deep draughts of rest, deep draughts of rest, and
    then
Again the red blood proudly pulsing on
Through the full veins, and heart and soul and
    all
Mine own once more !

AUGUSTUS.

                  You talk hexameters.
Gentle Vergilius pleaded so to me
With lovely lips like a woman's. He was weakish
Here, and his stomach followed on his head,
Poor lad, and so perforce we let him keep
With his kids and lambs and pretty manuscripts.
I did not know you were a poet, my friend,
Though, I remember now, you elegised Julius.

TIBERIUS.

A flame of the burnt-out candle ! All is ready,
Sire, for my parting hence to-night. I know
You will not keep your worn-out servant back.

AUGUSTUS.

You must not go.

TIBERIUS.

I beg you to say yes !

AUGUSTUS.

I will not have you go !

TIBERIUS.

I cannot stay !

AUGUSTUS.

You flout me ?

TIBERIUS.

Sire, I simply ask your leave
To let me go.

AUGUSTUS.

I will not give my leave.
You make too much of this. What is a woman ?

TIBERIUS.

You do distrust me, it would seem ?

AUGUSTUS.

I do.

TIBERIUS.

Then it were useless to keep me !   I must go !
What you would have me do I will do yet,
As I have promised.   Trust me, for you can.

AUGUSTUS.

You'd go against my wish.

TIBERIUS.

                              I thank you, sire.

AUGUSTUS.

There is my hand, a most unwilling hand.
Speak with your mother first.   I think this
    weak.

TIBERIUS.

I go, but I return, sire.   Trust in that.

AUGUSTUS.

That is because I must.   Write much, and oft.

TIBERIUS.

You shall not want for news of all I do.

AUGUSTUS.

You leave me to my burthen all alone.

TIBERIUS.

Ill help is worse than no help.   Sire, farewell !

AUGUSTUS.

Farewell.

TIBERIUS (*going, returns*).

Augustus

Must ne'er believe Tiberius does not love him,
As well as honour and revere.

AUGUSTUS.

I trust you !

Farewell, my friend. Go and return. I trust
you.

[TIBERIUS *going.*

SCENE II.

Rhodes. By the shore. The sea-temple of Aphro-
dite in the distance. Late afternoon. TI-
BERIUS, THRASYLLUS.

TIBERIUS.

(*Cymbals, pipes, and flutes within.*)
The music turns this way.

THRASYLLUS.

One of the processions

Up to the Temple of Aphrodite yonder.

TIBERIUS.

Stand back and let them pass. This country
worship

F

Comes nearer to the gods than the vain pomp
Our sceptic cities give us.   Think you not so?

THRASYLLUS.

Nearer to the devils, to the blind brute souls
That lie in plants and animals and stones.

TIBERIUS.

Ay, and in fragrant flowers and ferns and
    streams,
And this bright sea and beauteous earth of ours.

THRASYLLUS.

Yet you would have me leave all this, and go
To struggle with the insane lust of Rome?

TIBERIUS.

Ay, ay, but there are other things, my friend.
    [*Enter* PRIESTS, PRIESTESSES, *and* PEOPLE
     singing.

PRIESTS.

Down from the blue depths of heaven she fell,
The unborn babe from above.

PRIESTESSES.

Up from the blue depths of sea she came,
The goddess of life and love.

PRIESTS.

And the light, like a fragrant altar-flame,
Was round her on the sea's soft swell.

PRIESTESSES.

And the breezes sang their sweetest spell,
And the earth was glad of her as she came—

TOGETHER.

Aphrodite !

ALL.

Aphrodite, Aphrodite, Aphrodite !

[*They pass.*

TIBERIUS.

We were too close. The cymbals dinned mine
ears,
And flutes and pipes have made my blood run
thin.
So you'll not come ?

THRASYLLUS.

I have no quest in Rome.

TIBERIUS.

Yet Rome has consolations and delights.
There knowledge gathers to a splendid sun
And art and beauty swim, a sister moon,
Around this navel of the wondrous world.

Your friend, who goes now with a youth re-
    newed
To radiate power's concentric light and wield
Her flashing bolts, might he not serve life's cause
The better that you stood beside him there?

THRASYLLUS.

No, no, my track lies yonder from that orb,
Eastward and eastward wandering, till I find
The tree of death hard by the pools of peace.
I count no sun or moon so good as that.

TIBERIUS.

Is that the goal?   And I, too, in such time
When youth had sobered of the joys there are
With strength and beauty, I in those dusk
    lands
Have stood and questioned of dead stony gods.
Yea, and above me shone heaven's myriad lights,
And they seemed dead as well.   Yet I divined
Something beyond those emptied tenements,
A shade that flitted vainly, one last strain
Of jubilant music, one evanished flash,
And the great eyes of dead Semiramis!

THRASYLLUS.

Something there was, the last out-lingered relic

Of high and holy souls that once had more ;
But there the relic, elsewhere now we seek
Their living models.

TIBERIUS.

Seek, and do we find ?

THRASYLLUS.

We find, and seeking's over, and rest at last !

TIBERIUS.

Why, is that so ?   And you, are you not proud
To have the answer that our manhood ques-
tioned
And years maturer passed as idle game
For the delicate soul ?   Are you not therefore
proud ?

THRASYLLUS.

You smile at me.

TIBERIUS.

Nay, but you should be proud,
I'd think myself a god, if I knew what
The gods know, and the gods, it seems, are
proud,
At least they hold their tongues, and that is
pride.

THRASYLLUS.

Yes, we know all, and in that all is peace.

These men obscurely dreamed it.   Yet such
    knowledge
Brings but serenity and love, not pride.

TIBERIUS.

There is no answer there.

THRASYLLUS.

                    There is none, then !
We come—go whence we came, and that is good.
There is one life for all and many shapes.
Life is but restless effort till we know,
Eddies of tides before the full flood pours
On to his purpose.   This thing that we fear,
Death, is the one true life.   In the wild hours
Come pauses when we know this and are God.

TIBERIUS (pointing).

I'll build a causeway there, μὰ Κυνὰ, I will !
Why do you pull your hand in ?   Are you
    bitten ?
Scratch it ; 'tis pleasant.   Few things pleasanter
Than lie in the drowsy morn and scratch your-
    self.
I think the stars are emptied tenements,
Dead memories of life.

THRASYLLUS.

Perchance they are.
Yet in their courses there are miracles,
Immortal predeterminate influences,
Swaying the winds, driving the sea-currents,
Touching the flaming hills ! There is an ocean
With many isles and Etnas and strange forms
Of living creatures—men that live in trees,
Browsing on fruits. A temple, too, there is
Built of dead unknown hands, more marvellous
Than earth holds else. In those isles far away,
Where life is most profuse, that temple stands
Utterly alone, telling of patient peace.

ELECTRA (*within, singing*).

Phoebus is lord of the sea, he rises in light ;
His horses of gold, his chariot of gold, and his
     face so bright.
O that the god of day, the lord of the sea,
Would bend down his eyes but one moment
To me, even me !

TIBERIUS.

Thrasyllus, you're a wanderer of the tribe
Of old Herodotus. . . . She sings it sweetly . . .

Words, words !   We compass heaven and earth
    with words,
And rot fly-blown in the mud . . . She wants
    no lyre
With this air-music and the hymning sea. . . .
Did you ever love a woman ?
            THRASYLLUS.

               In past years
I sought for truth in them and the great God.
            TIBERIUS.
You never fished it up, though ? What, our
    plummets
Are all too short ?
            THRASYLLUS.

         Flesh is but flesh, no more !
        ELECTRA (*within, singing*).
Phœbus is lord of the sea ; and all day long
The chaunt of his praise goes up, radiant and
    strong !
O that the god of day, the lord of the sea,
Would speak with his lips but one word
To me, even me !
            TIBERIUS.
I fancy it is more.

ELECTRA (*within*).

Ah, ah !

MATHO (*within*).

Thou h-h-harpy !

Thou'lt say ah, ah, a-g-gain in a moment. Be
still.

No, not this time. I've g-got thee. Now say
ah !

ELECTRA (*within, screaming*).

Ah !

TIBERIUS.

A hawk is on our song-bird.

[*Enter* MATHO, *driving in* ELECTRA.

MATHO.

Sirs, g-good-day !

TIBERIUS.

What is this child ?

MATHO.

Sir, she's my slave.

THRASYLLUS.

Her mother

Ate honey on Hymettus then. She's Greek.

MATHO.

True, sir. Her mother, sir, she was Athenian,

Athenian suburban, a most un-g-grateful jade,
Who robbed me and ran away.

TIBERIUS.

Who are you ?

MATHO.

I ?

I am known vulgarly as Matho.

THRASYLLUS.

I think *I* know you.

TIBERIUS (*to* ELECTRA).

Where didst thou learn to sing, child ?

ELECTRA.

O, sir, sir.

O he has hurt mine arm so !   It's all bruised.
Poor thing !   Look at it !

TIBERIUS.

That's bad, very bad.

(*To* THRASYLLUS.)

Where's Artaxerxes ?   Seek him out for me.

THRASYLLUS (*going*).

That is mine use now—to seek Artaxerxes !

[*He goes out.*

MATHO.

Sir.

TIBERIUS.

Ha ?

MATHO.

I hope, sir—I anticipate—
I, in short, prog-g-g-nosticate that, so to say—

TIBERIUS.

What is your name ?

MATHO.

Sir, Matho, as I said—
Matho the c-coppersmith by denomination—
And this un-g-grateful, pretty, little dear
And charming g-girl's Electra, my slave's child.

ELECTRA.

O do not let him beat me, sir !   O do not !
He's very cruel, he's a wicked man !
To-day's a holiday !   He's shut the house up,
And where was I to go ?   I did no harm.

TIBERIUS.

Where is her mother—ha ?

MATHO.

Sir, Aphrodite
Is c-cognisant thereof ; none else !   Though that
Is rather, so to say, a flight of speech.
Her mother is concealed here, it may be,

In this c-cut-throat, immoral isle of Rhodes.
I do not say simply she *is*, you note, sir ?
For you, sir, who are, I see, of educ-cation
And c-comprehend the proper reservations,
Know truth is the τέλὸς.   Sir, to put it briefly,
I vegetate of ordinary in the town,
And, it being about the feast——

> [*Enter* ARTAXERXES.

TIBERIUS (*to* ARTAXERXES).

> Settle this stuttering crow.
I take the child.

ELECTRA.

> O, sir, I'm quite afraid.

TIBERIUS.

Thou needst not be afraid, my child.

ELECTRA.

> And will you
Send him away or take me with you, sir ?

MATHO.

Well, yes, g-good   man, yes, in   its   proper
   c-course
We will deliberate the matter, but . . .
O, yes, I see !   The master does not wish—
That   is,   he   does   not   prog-g-gnosticate . . .
   quite so.

Well, I will put the affair to you instead.
I vegetate of ordinary in the town,
And it being about——

TIBERIUS.

Take him away.

ARTAXERXES.

Come, sir,

We will remove a little farther.

MATHO.

But—

But, noble stranger, it would methinks be more,
So to say, satisfac-ctory, if you would listen
To what I've g-got to say !

ARTAXERXES.

Well, come on farther.

MATHO.

Yes, but you do not mark me what I say.
And being about the feast——

ARTAXERXES.

What sum you said ?

A little farther still.

MATHO.

Why so expeditious,
Mine oriental friend ?   I was about——

ARTAXERXES.

This way, this way.

[ARTAXERXES *and* MATHO *go out.*

TIBERIUS.

Well, well, my child, and where now wouldst
thou go?

ELECTRA.

With you, sir, please, for you have got kind
eyes,
And you will never beat me, nor get drunk
And kick and cuff me.

TIBERIUS.

I will never beat thee,
Nor yet get drunk and kick and cuff thee.

ELECTRA.

O,
Sir, I shall be so happy.

TIBERIUS.

How old art thou?

ELECTRA.

I do not know, but I am almost a woman.

TIBERIUS.

Where is thy mother?

ELECTRA.

Mother ?   She is dead.

She is gone far away over the sea.

TIBERIUS.

How long ago was that ?

ELECTRA.

A year ago.

The master beat her very much, and once
He cut her with a knife, and then she went.

TIBERIUS.

The master ?   That is Matho ?

ELECTRA.

The coppersmith.

He is very terrible.   He talks with spirits.
He has a black man made of smoke and flame
Under the fireplace.

TIBERIUS.

Is he thy father ?

ELECTRA.

No, he is not my father.

TIBERIUS.

Who's thy father ?

ELECTRA.

I do not know.   Mother and I came here

Years, years ago, and she was the master's wife.
They two slept in the bed.   I slept in a box.

TIBERIUS.

Where wast thou, then, before ?

ELECTRA.

I do not know.

In a great city with a beautiful hill
And marble places, white, and statues, and
    people.
I think they call it Athenai.   But the master
Would never speak of it without beating me.

TIBERIUS.

And was he never kind ?

ELECTRA.

Never at all !

I work and work all day about the house,
For he has no one else.   I do it out.
I cook the meals, and I cook very well,
Especially broths and stews.   On holidays
Sometimes he'll lock the house up and go forth,
And then I take my crusts down to the shore
And sit on the sand under the trees and sing.
Sometimes I follow the processions, too,
A long way off, for fear that he may catch me.

TIBERIUS.

Where didst thou learn thy song ?

ELECTRA.

Which song ?

TIBERIUS.

It runs :

" Phœbus is lord of the sea."

ELECTRA.

O, that song is a wonderful, beautiful song !
The ladies in white sing it in the temple there
Among the marble pillars.   I crept up
And listened to them.   There was one who sang
    it,
A great tall lady with red burnished hair
And a pale beautiful face.   The others sang
Together the first lines again, but she
Sang by herself.   She'd a deep voice like water.
I had to shut mine eyes and open my mouth,
When *she* sang.   I was hidden by a shrub.
I went there twice on holiday mornings.   Now
I'll never hear her sing again, I fear.

TIBERIUS.

Lo, in the sea the bright sun is just dipped,
And there lies Rome, and life for thee and me.
Do not cry, dear.

G

ELECTRA.

No, I'll not cry about it,
If I may go with you.   I do not think
You'll make me work so hard as the master did.

TIBERIUS.

Thou shalt not work at all, unless thou list,
But as thou pleasest shalt do all day long.

ELECTRA.

Holiday all day long?   But then, who is it
That makes your broths and stews, and cleans
        the house ?

TIBERIUS.

I have others who do that.

ELECTRA.

                    You are very rich ?

TIBERIUS.

Yes, I am rich.

ELECTRA.

            Richer than the master is ?
He has got a pot of money under the rafters.
I know about it.

TIBERIUS.

            Richer than even the master.

ELECTRA.

Holiday every day?   Did you say that ?

TIBERIUS.

Yes, I said that.

ELECTRA.

O Aphrodite, what
A lucky girl I am !   And do you think
That I shall clean the pots, and scrub the house,
And make the bed up, and shall brush and cook,
Not any more ?

TIBERIUS.

I think so.

ELECTRA.

Then I'm sure
My hands will get quite white in time. I'm sure,
If I could have the chance, I'd make them white.
It must be heavenly, sure, to have white hands !
O Aphrodite, I shall be beautiful
When I have got white hands.

TIBERIUS.

My dear, thou seemest
To me already beautiful.

ELECTRA.

Dost think so ?
That's very strange.   But is that true thou
    sayest ?

TIBERIUS.

It is very true.   Be good as well, and then
Thou wilt be happy always.

ELECTRA.

O, I'll be good,

O, I'll be good, so good.   It is very easy,
I'm sure, when you've not got to work, to be
      good.

TIBERIUS.

We do not find it quite so.

ELECTRA.

And am I

To come with thee and be thy—slave instead?

TIBERIUS..

To come with me and do just as thou wilt.

ELECTRA.

And dost thou think that I might dress in white,
All, all in white, and sit by the sea and sing?

TIBERIUS.

Yes, thou shalt dress in white in a few hours,
And sit and sing in a marble portico
Among the pillars as the stars come out.

ELECTRA.

O, but I think I'll die before all that!
Let us make haste!

[*Re-enter* THRASYLLUS.

TIBERIUS.

Straightway, my child, in a moment.
Well, then, Thrasyllus, do we part here now?
You still hold to it? You will leave me?

THRASYLLUS.

Yes;
It will be better so.

TIBERIUS.

Remember, friend,
That was no empty phrase I made for you.
If ever you should have a need of me,—
If ever you should have a care to come,—
I am there and wishful to do aught I may
For the sincerest. . . . But farewell, Thrasyllus.
I love, I value you. Your hand. Farewell.

ELECTRA (*to* TIBERIUS, *going*).

Why look'st thou sad? Thine eyes are full of
_ tears.
Do not be sad. I will be so, so good!

TIBERIUS.

I'm smiling, dear. Sing to me as we go.

[TIBERIUS *and* ELECTRA *go out.*

THRASYLLUS.

But there are hours when from the Delphic past
Strange exhalations and reverberant dreams

Afflict the soul swung in the grated present,
While the dim future, like a lover woman
Lain heavy on the limbs, pores on the face.
The happiness of sweet forgotten dreams,
And dreadful forms, the visible shapes of thought,
Passion's unknown monstrosities of love,
Low breaths of life and deep delicious calm,
Alternate as the radial winds of storm
Driving around the centre.

ELECTRA (*without, singing*).

Phœbus is lord of the sea, he rises in light,
His horses of gold, his chariot of gold, and his
    face so bright.
O that the god of day, the lord of the sea,
Would bend down his eyes but one moment
To me, even me.

THRASYLLUS.

    There's more joy
In still green places with the heaven's high sun,
And night's first hush with moon and clustering
    stars,
Than all the tortuous boskage and the plains
And mankind crowding homes. No, never-more
That poisoned bait shall draw me! O fair star,

Fairest and first, behold me, for I go,
I go to where life's fatal outcries cease,
Where man and strife are whelmed in peace and
    God.

    Electra (*within, singing farther off*).

Phœbus is lord of the sea ; and all day long
The chaunt of his praise goes up radiant and
    strong—
O that the god of day, the lord of the sea,
Would speak with his lips but one word . . .

                   (*Dying away*).

    (THE SCENE CLOSES.)

ACT III.

Rome. A room in TIBERIUS' *house on the Palatine. Laurel-crowned busts of* JULIUS CÆSAR
and AUGUSTUS. *Windows showing Rome
without. Morning.* SEJANUS, ELECTRA.

SEJANUS.

Where is thy master, dear?

ELECTRA (*with a cithara*).

I have no master.

I am a free girl.

There! Are not those notes pretty? Listen
again.

La, la, la, la, la, la! I learn so quick!

The rain and clouds are gone. I am so glad!

When I can play, I'll play and sing together,

For I have many tunes here in my head,

But, when I make and sing them, I forget.

Those silly birds shriek so in the vestibules.

SEJANUS.

Who art thou, child?

ELECTRA.

Who am I ?   I'm Electra,
And, as I am full grown, I'm not a child.

[*Taking his hand.*

A pretty ring that.

SEJANUS.

Well, Electra, listen.

ELECTRA (*playing*).

I'd soonest listen to the notes.

SEJANUS.

Perhaps,
But this I speak of is important.

ELECTRA.

So

Are the notes.   And when I've learned them
    and can play
A song complete to him, I am to have
All sorts of things.   I will not tell you what.
Do you go to the circus and the games ?
La, la, la, la !   I've four tame nightingales.

SEJANUS (*at the door-curtains*).

Ripe woman playing child and meaning it
Is an old venture now.   Yet what's behind ?
The mature Siren loses her cruelty.

I do confess that, looking thus upon her,
I find myself a man and her a woman.

ELECTRA (*playing and singing*).
          Into the sky to the sun
          (For the spring's begun)
          The lark turns round,
Soaring and singing, away from the ground.

SEJANUS.

Here's the good Artaxerxes, the stone man
Who does what's bid him like an arbalast.
The bright brave cloudless blue and golden sun
Have caught me also.   I could laugh aloud.

[*Enter* ARTAXERXES.

ARTAXERXES.

My lord, a happy morrow.   The Prince bids you
Await him here ; he comes immediately.

SEJANUS.

He honours his poor friend too much. . . .

ELECTRA.
                              You two,
Why do you stand like uncles at a funeral ?
You're very shy.   I think you must be modest,
You stranger lord.   Look at him how he's
     blushing.

SEJANUS.

Your bright eyes blind me, pretty bird, perhaps.
Is it decided yet, then, Artaxerxes,
Whether he goes back to Illyricum ?

ARTAXERXES.

'Tis thought so.   News came in to us last night
Of discontent and mutinous demands
Made by the soldiers.

SEJANUS.

          I heard, too, of trouble
In the Cisalpina province.   All has seemed
Unhinged since Varus met his bloody fall.
The state is like a rider that's been thrown,
And his lost nerve shakes in the saddle.   Yet
Tiberius and Germanicus left things well
Before Rome joyed at their Dalmatian triumphs.
It was a rigorous business.

ARTAXERXES.

          That is so.

SEJANUS.

Has the Prince heard of Drusus yet ?   Believe
   me
It came near to a scandal.   All I could
I did to save and shield him.

ARTAXERXES.

               The Prince has heard,
And thanks you well. His son is in the country
At his villa with his wife, and writes of you.
The Empress, too, spoke of her gratitude.

SEJANUS.

I trusted that the Emperor might not hear it.
It would incense him. He's been quick of
     temper,
They tell me, ever since the Varus loss.
And at the Court, what of Germanicus ?

ARTAXÉRXES.

Germanicus stands at the summit, sir.

SEJANUS.

He gets there by selection, it would seem !
'Tis strange such things should happen in such
     ways !
Fortune told never yet a tale like his !
Young Gaius Cæsar in Armenia,
And Lucius at Massilia, in one year,
So young, so strong, both dead, who seemed all
     life !
Then Postumus adopted : then expelled
With his sister Julia ; then the Emperor

Adopts the Prince, but passes by his son,
The Empress' darling, for the nephew who,
Adopted by the Prince, weds Agrippina,
The daughter of that Prince's exiled wife,
The hapless Julia,
And Fortune crowns their wedlock with a boy,
Gaius the soldiers dote on as Caligula !
Thrice-blest Germanicus ! Not once in ages
Doth peerless worth reach thus the peerless
    place !
But neither the Empress nor the Prince, I doubt,
Is over-joyous with the applauded pair ?
The Prince perhaps remembers Julia,
And Julia's Julia, and misdoubts a vestal !
And then Livilla, though she likes her brother,
" The great Germanicus," may well like better
Her husband, the brave Drusus we all cleave to
The more for his hot, manly, honest faults.

                    ARTAXERXES.
Livilla is your friend, my lord, staunch friend.
The Prince remarked so. In these dual factions
That rend the Court for Drusus and his
    cousin . . .
The Prince is coming.

SEJANUS (*aside*).
                    I did not hear his steps.
These quiet men have ears like cats.   I fear
I somewhat foolishly talked with him.
                    ELECTRA.
                                        O hey,
You there, you stranger lord, you're blushing
        again.
                    SEJANUS.
I would not blush if we were in the dark,
And——
                    ELECTRA.
            Fiddle-faddle.
                            [*Enter* TIBERIUS.
                    TIBERIUS.
                        So, my good Sejanus !
                ARTAXERXES (*aside*).
He takes him by the arm—now round his
        shoulder—
And leads him to the casement.   There's more
        here
Than I had thought of.   It may chance that
        yet
This clever fool may mount upon men's
        shoulders.

What matters it ?   I am the same to all.
Electra, come !   The Prince would be alone
Here with Sejanus.

ELECTRA.

Oh, but he's a nice man !
I'll stop and play.   You must not bully me.
Now don't you try to bully me !

ARTAXERXES.

Stop, if you please.

[*He goes out.*

ELECTRA (*playing and singing softly*).

A little baby, a little baby,
O the gods to give me one !
Its little hands, its little feet,
It's little eyes and lips so sweet,
As it sucks and will not be done,
My little baby, my little baby !

TIBERIUS.

There's my good child.   But now thou'lt sing
   no more.
Thou dost distract us.   Go within, dear.

ELECTRA.

Well,
Well, I don't like people who are cross to me !

TIBERIUS.

We are not cross.   Sejanus is all smiles.
We stopped to hear thy song.   Now we have
        work.
Be a good girl.

ELECTRA.

                And wilt thou give me, then,
That star thou hast promised?   I'll wear that
        to-night.

TIBERIUS.

Tell Artaxerxes of it.   He will give thee
The money for it.   Go and buy it now.

ELECTRA.

Then kiss me.   I don't like people who go out
Not kissing other people !

                        [TIBERIUS *kisses her.*

ELECTRA.

                    How do I play ?

TIBERIUS.

Thou playest better every day, I think.

ELECTRA.

I think so too.   Go not till I return.
Good-day, sir.

Sejanus.

Good-day, madam.

[Electra *goes out.*

Tiberius.

Indeed, I have much happiness in the child.

She's as the sunshine to me and the flowers.

I sometimes thank this bitter earth for her.

Sejanus.

I never saw her before, but we all know

The Prince's beautiful Greek.   Her fame and
    Helena's

Stand ever equal in the deathless verse.

Tiberius.

Is the epigram so known ? · 'Tis only poets

Can woo the women.

Sejanus.

The poets and the princes !

Tiberius.

That is bad news we have from Cisalpina.

Retain the guards in readiness to start

At any hour.   I'll face the trouble myself.

Will you come with me ?

Sejanus.

O believe most readily.

H

TIBERIUS.

We'll hold command between us.
                    SEJANUS.

                              O my Prince,
You overwhelm me !
                    TIBERIUS.

                    Tell me whom you'll take
As master of your horse, when you have chosen.
                    SEJANUS.

There is Chœrea.   He is young, but yet
A brilliant soldier, and a politician.
                    TIBERIUS.

Nowadays we need the two.   He stands ap-
     pointed.
Macro is mine.   What is it that you meant
Of Agrippina in your letter ?
                    SEJANUS.

                              I have it
From a sure friend in the camp (his name's
     Getulicus.
You do not know him ?   He's both shrewd and
     honest)
That at the public tables with the staff
She spoke of you offensively.

TIBERIUS.

And Germanicus ?

SEJANUS.

Sat silently and shook his head at it.
It is the common scandal that her ways
With some of the officers are bold and free.
She laughs and says she likes a handsome man.
Then there's Asinius——

TIBERIUS.

Gallus ?   Ha, what of Gallus ?

SEJANUS.

He writes her secret letters, and she him.
Getulicus has suspicions of them both.

TIBERIUS.

Gallus, beware ! beware lest some day yet
Thou smart for many things !   Well, that is
    kind—
Your friend is kind to watch so o'er mine in-
    terest,
And I shall not forget it.   You know Augustus
Comes here an hour from noon ?   I think all
    Rome
Sees he is weak and ailing, but few dream
The very flame of life is flickering in him.

TIBERIUS.

SEJANUS.

The Emperor dying ?   Is Augustus dying ?

TIBERIUS.

Death sounds no word for such a man as he !
Yet is he leaving us.

SEJANUS.

I had not thought of it.

TIBERIUS.

Scarcely had I, who saw it, dared to say
Even to myself that it was close.

SEJANUS.

And he ?

TIBERIUS.

Augustus is not one to turn himself
From what is destined. His clear eyes have
    viewed it,
Facing, surpassing it, while we looked elsewhere.

SEJANUS.

Olympian Jupiter, divine Augustus !

[*They turn to the busts.   Enter* SCRIBONIA.

TIBERIUS.

Scribonia ?

SCRIBONIA.

It is I, my lord.

TIBERIUS.

Scribonia ? . . .

But you are ill and weak.　Sit here.　Nay, lady,
Speak not at once.　Wait ; we will talk anon,
Some water and wine, Sejanus.　Bring it thy-
　　self. . . .　　　　　　　　　[SEJANUS *goes out.*
These last few days' hot wind has killed us all,
Till the cold change came with the storm last
　　night.
You have been travelling in them?
　　　　　　　　　[*She would kiss his hand.*
　　　　　　　　　　　No, no !　Nay,
Be comforted.　Do not weep.　Rest.

SCRIBONIA.

Tiberius

Always gentle and kind !　But let me speak.

TIBERIUS.

No, no, not yet !　Wait till Sejanus comes.
A little wine and water and some fruit
Will make you strong again.　Be comforted.
　　　　　　　　　[*Re-enter* SEJANUS.
You see he is more careful than I was.
He has brought you cakes.

SCRIBONIA.

A little water, then.

TIBERIUS.

And just this sup of wine to show the colour
In sunlight.   And now drink—nay, drink it all;
And eat, however little.   We want food
As well as drink to work this body of ours.

SCRIBONIA.

That is enough.   I thank you.

(*To* SEJANUS.)

I thank you, sir.

[SEJANUS *goes out.*

Tiberius, I . . .

TIBERIUS.

Speak on.   Be not afraid.
Lady Scribonia has no cause to fear
To speak where all who listen honour her
And love her.

SCRIBONIA.

Julia—Julia has left the villa.
She somehow slipped the servants three nights
        past.
I've travelled night and day
To get here to you first.   No, no, Augustus—

He has not heard it yet.   What will he do?
I am afraid—I am terrified for her!

TIBERIUS.

Where is she now?   In Rome?   Here?

SCRIBONIA.

That I know not!
O the poor child!   She is sadly, sadly changed!
She is pale, and gaunt, and wanders like a ghost
About the rooms all day; and in the nights
She rises in her sleep, and peers at the moon,
And moves the jars.   I follow her for hours.
I fear lest she may do some desperate thing.
Sometimes in rage she falls, frothing at the
    mouth,
Staring up with fixed eyes, crunching her teeth.
I weep and wipe the wet from her poor lips.
Anon, she plays and talks as she did as a child.
It breaks my heart to hear her prattle and sing.
Then, when she's slept, she wakes and forgets it
    all.
She is half mad.   Tiberius, O Tiberius . . .

TIBERIUS.

Speak on, Scribonia.   What is it that you
Would have me do?

SCRIBONIA.

    Augustus—think—his anger !
I am terrified.   He may imprison—kill her—
Smother or poison her, my child, my baby,
My helpless Julia !   O but, Tiberius,
Think not she's wholly bad, not wicked.   No ;
She is generous and brave, I'm sure.   Believe
    me !
She has done ill, but she has never hid it,
But made it seem the worse by blazoning all.
You will not let him kill her ?   He hates her so
By now.   I thought he'd strangle her himself
The last time that he saw her.   That was when
You were at Rhodes.   O, it was terrible !
She faced him to the last.   Tiberius,
Intercede—save her—let her not be killed,
My poor, poor Julia !   Hush !   Hark !   She ?
    she ? here?

JULIA I. (*within*).
Stop me ?   You will be doing well to stop me.
Stand back, I am Julia, Augustus' daughter !

SEJANUS (*within*).
But, lady——

JULIA I.

But ! (*She draws the curtains.*)

[*Enter* JULIA. *Re-enter* SEJANUS.

(*A long silence.*)

I am come,
Tiberius, to say a few words to you
And to my father. Do you know that I
Have been an exile and a prisoner now
For fourteen years ? And do you know that I
Have asked—have begged—besought—entreated
    —prayed—
Knelt—cringed—Yes, it is I have cringed and
    knelt !—
For freedom, and the answer, the one answer,
Silence, for fourteen years silence ! Prayers,
    tears,
Despairs, abjections, agonies—and silence !
'Tis thus Augustus and Tiberius treat
A woman ! Say, why do you torture me
To death by fractions of inches ? Do you fear
    me ?
How you must hate me !
My woman hung herself, and she did well,
But I am somewhat tamed. Look you, this hand

Is like the skeleton's that my body is.
I am devoured with fever.   The little blood
Left in my flaccid veins is fire.   Dark death
Glowers brooding at me in the horrible nights.
No one would kiss me.   Who would let these
     bones
Clutch them in love's embrace?   I am very
     weary.
Husband, you have small need of jealousy.
I once was Julia.   Now I am no more.
Let me go free.   My very voice is like
A voice heard in a tomb, hollow and lifeless,
One dreary wail!   Why must I die in a tomb?
Let me go free! . . .

SEJANUS (*to* TIBERIUS).
               My lord, at any moment
Augustus comes.   The hour is past already.

TIBERIUS.
Ah!

SEJANUS.
Shall I go?   Attempt to stop him?

TIBERIUS.
               No, stay.

JULIA I.

Ha, what was that you said ?   I still can hear.
Augustus, then, is coming ?   Be it so !
I will wait and see him.

SCRIBONIA.

O Julia, Julia,
Do not stop here !   Let us go—quickly.

JULIA I.

Mother,
I did not fear that snake, though it could crush
    me
And though it had what nature will not give,
Poisonous fangs as well.   Now, poisoned,
    crushed,
I do not fear it !   Cease to entreat me so.
Never weep there and kneel.   Be more proud,
    mother,
To those who've wronged and tortured us.   I
    come,
I come to ask my freedom from these two
Who've had revenge on me for fourteen years.
I think that is enough for even a father
And husband.

TIBERIUS.

Lady Julia does me wrong.
I had no word in this her banishment.
I have no word now in her prisoning.

JULIA I.

You say so. I believe you. O, but what right
Had you to banish—to imprison me,
You, or my father, or the gods themselves ?
That I had loved this man or that who was not
My lawful mate ? that I had laughed and sung
And passed some pleasant hours ? Tiberius,
You have a mother, and are aware how you
Did get a stepfather. You know that man.
One of his friends, Mœcenas, who had done
    him
Inestimable service, had a wife
He loved and who loved him, and this was why
He took that wife and used her. As for me,
He gave me to Marcellus, to Agrippa,
To you, to any one his statescraft wished for,
As men give horse or dog. He has used us all !
Could you demand my faith to you, or I
Your faith to me ? Have you—has he—has any
    man

Been of a life so pure, that he can dare
To arrogate the judging of a woman ?
No, not of a harlot !

SEJANUS (*aside*).

Why, this is Klutaimnestra !
The superb actress-wanton, incarnate Rome !

JULIA I.

You answer nothing ?

TIBERIUS.

Nothing.   I regret
Your   wretchedness.   I   never   wished   you
wretched.

SEJANUS (*to* TIBERIUS).

There is a stir in the passage.   He is here.

SCRIBONIA.

Come, come, child !   O Tiberius, ask her you.
Let us go out.   O, come, my Julia, come !

JULIA I.

I stay.

[*Enter* AUGUSTUS.

AUGUSTUS.

Ha ! . . . You—thou—miserable—infect—

SEJANUS (*to* TIBERIUS).

He will fall down.

AUGUSTUS (*to* SEJANUS).

       No, no, I do not want you.

Some of that water and a little wine.

Tiberius, tell those women they're to go.

JULIA I.

Has he the palsy that he shakes so ?   This

Augustus ?   He will slobber presently.

TIBERIUS.

Will you not come, lady ?   Come ; 'twill be

   best.

What we can do to win your freedom, be

You sure, we all will do.

JULIA I.

              I stay !

SCRIBONIA.

Julia——

JULIA I.

   Be silent.   I'm as fierce

As that chalked dotard was.

AUGUSTUS.

         She dares me, then ?

Thou execrable shame of my fame and line !

Cancer that didst eject two cancers fouler.

Even than thyself, out, out !   Know this, know

   this :

Thy spawn shall die, those two incestuous toads,
Thy Julia and Postumus. Open not thy mouth!
Wilt thou begone?
Infamous, execrable hag, harpy, cancer,
Shame of my name, execrable incestuous——

JULIA I. (*laughing*).

Ha, ha! Old, stuttering mask, repeat it all!
Go through it all and yet again! (*To* SEJANUS.)
Off, man!
Wilt come betwixt a tigress and a snake?

SCRIBONIA.

O keep between them! They will kill each
other!

JULIA I.

Look at that spitting cat that is Augustus!
The virulent driveller they call a god!

AUGUSTUS.

Somebody stop her.

SEJANUS.

Lady, retire.

JULIA I.

Retire?

Not till I wring his life out at his gums
And skinny throat!

AUGUSTUS (*waving his hand*).

    Horrible, horrible, horrible !

      [*He faints.*

TIBERIUS.

Lady, you harm yourself as much as him
And all of us. Come. Let me lead you. Come.

    JULIA I (*at the curtains*).

Will you use force ? Claudius, I once did love
    you.
Why did you drive my love back on my hate ?
I could love more in a minute than in a life
Vapid Vipsania with her baby eyes.
If you had been but kind, I had been happy,
As I have never been. That night, remember,
I would have stabbed thee. But thou, my hero,
    caughtest
With thy strong dexterous left my woman's
    wrist,
And eyed'st me helpless. I hated and adored
    thee !

    SEJANUS (*with* AUGUSTUS, *aside*).

She'll kiss him in an instant on the mouth !
She scents imperial carrion and would be em-
    press.

Gods, she is glorious with her bright red lips.
Fever or rouge, I'd kiss them !

JULIA I.

I have suffered so much ! O be kind ! Forget—
Forgive !

TIBERIUS.

I have forgiven and forgotten.

JULIA I.

I have but a short time to live.   Forgive !
Let me return.

TIBERIUS.

Lady, it cannot be.

AUGUSTUS.

There yet ? is she there yet ?   Ha, gods, I think
I am Emperor no more, and what I say
Is empty air.

TIBERIUS.

Come, lady.   You must come.

[*Enter* LIVIA.

JULIA I.

O, I curse you, curse you all !   Die—perish—
  rot—
Rot while you yet are living, all of you,
As I have done.   My bitter, eternal curse
On thee, grey murd'rous spider, and you all,

I

The flies of his infamous web. Decay and perish,
Before the tranquil hours of happy death
Remove the shuddering senses. Men and women,
Children, each root and twig of the foul tree,
Wither upon the world's avenging altar
You call a throne! Palsy, disease, and madness,
Madness, madness, madness consume you all!
My brain bursts. O, O, O!

      [SCRIBONIA *leads* JULIA *out.*
     AUGUSTUS (*muttering*).

Gag him. Shut up his mouth and strangle him. . . .
Varus, give back my legions to me, Varus!
So many men laid dead for the wolves and crows,
So many, many men, so young and strong!
Give back my legions, give me back my legions! . . .
I see Agrippa's eye stare through the veil.
He still will warn me . . . Arrogant? No, these hours
I have spent begging humbly in the streets.

LIVIA.

He faints, he faints again! Quick, water, and
    wine!

Sire, husband, speak. He's gone. Open it
    quick.

Cut with a knife. Give him some air. He's
    gone. . . .

No, he revives. Get back, and draw the
    curtains.

SEJANUS (*aside*).

Death like a thundercloud hangs o'er the city.

That changed lugubrious voice sounded from
    Hades.

AUGUSTUS.

That will suffice . . . Thanks, thanks. I am
    better . . . Thanks . . .

I can stand up. I am myself . . . My friends,

Forget what late has passed, for aye. Draw
    back.

Sejanus too.

I have my death, Tiberius, yea, my death.

This only brings it closer. A mad rage

Possessed me. I forget my moderation.

Then it is time I went.   I am calm now.

I have not much to say.   All thou should'st
  know

Thou knowest.   I have hidden nothing from
  thee.

I never hoped for such a man as thou art

To work our purpose with.   I thank the gods

That Julius and Augustus find a third

Here in Tiberius.   Often have I doubted

That thou would'st spoil thyself.   My son, thou
  hast

Thy share of witless hours.

Thou hast not that sure knowledge of men's
  beings

That I had.   Thou hast too much heart in thee:

It colours even thy mind.   Beware of that.

'Twas mine to know the man to do the work.

Farewell now.   Come to-night to sup.   Thy
  mother

Would have thee with us.   Livia, come.   Farewell,

Sejanus.   I shall see you, sir, ere long.

I lean on my wife's arm now, my good wife!

        [AUGUSTUS, LIVIA, *and* TIBERIUS *go out.*

SEJANUS.

He's a dead man, and Julia's vehement spirit
Flares in the socket. Safe, untouched sails by
The eagle empire. We are on the brink
Of the great eastward hills and through the dark
Envisage the young dawn. Germanicus
Upon the Rhine may answer the Empress' hate
With the bold stroke for all that's his and ours,
But he hath an imperious wife whose clamour
Will ever make them spill what they would
    drink.
Revolt in Cisalpina threatens ; there
Sejanus goes the Prince's chartered colleague.
Danger doth hedge us like a gathering storm
Round a bright isle of light, but that isle's rock,
And breasts and beats all winds and waves can
    do it.
Many a time my youth
Did dream and scheme of such an hour as this
With such a man. The man and hour are
    come !

                    [*Re-enter* TIBERIUS.

TIBERIUS.

I never saw him greater than to-day,

From that unheard-of outburst passing to
A calm so wonderful. Such weakness showed
    him
To be a man : such strength to be a god !

SEJANUS.

Augustus is—Augustus.   He stands alone,
As Julius stood, none equal and none like,
The tutelary influences of this house
And Rome and the world !
          [They stand looking at the busts.

TIBERIUS.

That is the very truth.
I once thought Julius greater. Now T know
    not.
Augustus wrought his work as a god would.
Like the great sun, he lingers as he sets.
Sejanus, there's the necessity on us
Of the broad spreading of the morrow morn.
Day follows night, night follows day, though
    gods
Perish as the sea-whelmed sun or the fallen
    moon.
Our grim work faces us. I think you know it.

We have often talked together. This rain-
    cloud

Within the north is nought. The German
    troops

May bluster and shake the shrouds, but they'll
    prove true.

Germanicus is true. The real work's here

In Rome. I hate this city. I breathe not free
    in it.

It hath a fever prevalent that consumes me,

Lays bare my nerves, and makes mine acts weak
    haste

That should be quiet and strong like Nature's
    laws.

             SEJANUS.

Something I have observed of this.

             TIBERIUS.

                        Sejanus,

There stands between the peace and power of
    the world

A gang of old assassin-thieves, these ruthless,

Greedy, lustful Roman aristocrats !

Augustus held them down ; his moderation

Seemed more than mercy to their guilty dread.

Now they take heart again. The stake is huge,
I see their eyes aglitter, and, when his hand
Is raised, they make their last most tigerish leap
To thrust the Emperor from his armoured watch
And seize the world again, their helpless prey
For robbery and crime. They shall never
    do it !
Sejanus, there is but one word for them,
That word's extermination ! Man by man
Calmly and coldly we will cull them out
As we would weeds—unwearied trap and slay
    them
As we would vermin ! They are the world's
    curse.

SEJANUS.

The world's curse, as the Prince is the world's
    cure.

TIBERIUS.

But how shall I do this in the mad city
That whirls my head like wine ? I'd not be
    cruel.
I would be evenly just, nor shed one blood-drop
Or more, or less, than the thing needs. A man,
Intelligent, strong to be my hand in Rome,

The very centre of the storm of power,

While that my soul, safe in its calm removed,

Dispensed their fate to them. That is my
dream.

For I am weak too.. Heart and mind in me

Stretch for dear hands to bear with me this
burthen.

Give me communion with an equal soul !

Thou hadst a wife, I know, who left a daughter,

Helpless bequest of what was dearer to thee

Than anything less than heart, mind, soul and
all,

And I, I had a brother and a wife

Who made that up ; and both, and both are
gone.

Who is there—who—

Can take his stand with me, Fate's arbiter

And wielder of the thunder-bolts I forge ?

                    SEJANUS.

Your nephew and adoptive son.

                    TIBERIUS.

                              Germanicus ?

I love Germanicus ; he it is, I think,

Who yet shall work our terrible purposes

To golden glad fulfilment, Drusus' boy !
Perchance my son, too, yet may cool his blood
And in the broad to-morrow do his duty.
But there is one closer and dearer to-day,
Companion, comrade, friend !   And who is he ?

SEJANUS.

I cannot dare to guess or speak his name.

TIBERIUS.

Then I who know must utter it to thee—
Sejanus !

SEJANUS (kneeling).

O mine Emperor.

TIBERIUS (raising him).

O my friend !

ACT IV.

Rome. A room in the house of Sejanus. A large door and balcony behind, showing the gardens and Rome, illuminated in the moonlight. CHÆREA, AELIA.

AELIA.

I fear, and yet I know not whom or what.
My heart, too, is not wholly in all this.
O my Chærea, treason is a word
Of a foul touch, and what's ingratitude
But the infernal snake that bites the hand
That draws it kindly from the snow and warms
    it?
The Prince has ever been most good to us.
If now my father's name of great Sejanus
Sits on an equal throne beside the Prince's,
Tiberius raised it there. I think he loves him.

CHÆREA.

Aelia, in the fierce game of life and power,
We play not as we will but as we must.

Each knows his counter-gamester stakes his all,
And what is talk of love and gratitude
And nobleness and virtue and such names,
But coins that are for him whose hand can grasp
    them ?
Tiberius played and won as we play now,
Who yet may win or lose.

AELIA.

                I would I thought it.

CHÆREA.

He loved his wife Vipsania. Did that stand
But he divorced her, and, with jealousy
Most mean, destroyed the husband that she
    took
To comfort her repulse, letting her die
Desolate ? Then his second wife, once used
So as to make him guardian of her sons,
Augustus' heirs, what did he do with her ?
Her squalid exile answers ! Next, these boys,
Gaius and Lucius, how got they their deaths
That were the steps for him up to the summit?
Augustus, passing by Tiberius' son,
The dissolute Drusus, chose Germanicus,
The elder Drusus' child. And what of him ?

Though he had quelled the German legionaries
Who'd make him Emperor when Augustus
    passed
Up to the gods—though he had saved the state
And served it as none other man had done,
The breath of dull dishonour blew on him
With such a pestilential influence
That he dies poisoned by it in Syria,
And Drusus wins his place. Why, look, his
    mother,
This monster's mother, her who'd given him all,
He used and flung aside. Her title even,
Augusta, left her by the Emperor's will,
Her son contests : then charges her with the
    murder
Through Piso of Germanicus. O ye gods !
That such a man . . .

AELIA.

I've heard these hideous tales : yet seems he
    kind.

CHÆREA.

Kind ? He's a ruthless, an infuriate serpent,   ˙
Sucking our heart and strength and body and
    brain.

Thy father would have married Drusus' widow,
Livilla, as thou know'st.   He would not let him.

AELIA.

Livilla ?   I could never like her, Cassius,
Though I tried much.   I fear she is not honest.

CHÆREA.

Then with poor Postumus, why, say, must he
    kill him ?

AELIA.

'Twas said Augustus willed it, for some crime
Committed—

CHÆREA.

           Years ago, forgotten quite,
A mere pretext !   Yes, he's in sheer perfection
The hangman hypocrite.   Look at the scorn of
    him,
Through his Augustan aped humility,
Muttering in Greek there in the Senate House :
" O creatures born and greedy to be slaves ! "
The Scipios and the Lamias slaves to him !
They scorn him : so he slays them, and they
    scorn him !
And what's so mean he will not stoop him to ?
Insult and goad a woman, till she weeps :

Then call her water-pot ! Let her flash wrath,
And he'll cry traitress. Or if at last, worn out,
She ask a husband to protect her years,
He'll tell the world that noble Agrippina,
Peerless Germanicus' spouse, has wanton blood !
He is a devil !

AELIA.

Speak no more of him !
I grow already to dream I see his eyes
With their fixed stare like statues', and his face
Silent, inscrutable, and dreadful brows.

[*Enter* CALIGULA *behind.*

CHÆREA.

Ay, he'd disgrace his mother, her, Augusta,
The hand that shaped him from pool-bottom
    mud
Into the mould of the world's idol. And why?
For a few kind words, yea, for a woman's heart
That was a mother's and pitied Agrippina,
The exiled daughter of the exiled corpse
That once gave glorious vision to all Rome,
Augustus' and Agrippa's Julia !
O virtuous, philosophic, stoic saint,
O butcher of Rome's noblest, bravest, best,

Racked with a hundred pains and puling ills,
Hating to live and shuddering still to die,
O loathsome lecherous Capræan beast,—

AELIA (*covering her face*).
O cease, cease, Cassius, cease !

CHÆREA.

Ah, you, my lord !
I did not see you.   Aelia, sweet love,
Leave us a moment.   Wilt thou seek thy father
And bring him to us? We would speak together.
                    [AELIA *goes out.*
My lord, you look not quite so well as you do
Of ordinary.

CALIGULA.
No, no ! I have a headache.
Your speech . . .

CHÆREA.
'Twas nothing.   Thus I do entrap them.
I urge them so into extreme desires,
That every step they make and we draw back
Widens the gulf that saves us, swallows them !

CALIGULA.
That's very clever.

CHÆREA.

Yours was the hint I drew from.

CALIGULA.

Well, yes, I hinted.   But I fear, Chærea,
It is not altogether honest, moral,
And beautiful.

CHÆREA.

I want that balance you . . .

CALIGULA.

No, no, I do not doubt but it is best.
But it is rare that what is best, you know,
Is beautifullest—as with our great Augustus.
You may remember how I put it thus
In mine oration at the obsequies?

CHÆREA.

Not Cicero could have put it so.   No, never!
Since all Rome flashed to wrath and retribution
Where Julius lay and over him Antonius
Spake words and flames, have human ears so
      tingled
As those that heard you that sad day, my lord!

CALIGULA.

Germanicus, my father, was the prince
Of soldiers : I, perhaps, can speak the better.

K

CHÆREA.

You speak. as none can speak in these poor
    times.
We are degenerate.

CALIGULA.

We are not what we were.
Our fathers were a mightier race.

CHÆREA.

My lord,
Your princely pardon, but the time now presses,
And danger's everywhere till we are done.
Since I left Capreæ has nought transpired ?
The Prince . . . he still believes . . . he does
    not think . . .

CALIGULA.

No, he believes.
But had it been a few hours later when
You told him, we were all undone, even I—
Most dreadful !   But he said to me that night
That he was proud to have so many protectors.
He smiled.   His smile is often most unpleasant.
It makes your head go round.   I learned from
    him
You scarce had left him when some other came

(I cannot tell you who) and gave the plan
In full, and then again on the next morning
A third !

CHÆREA.

One was the man who sent the scroll
Electra found under his pillow and warned me.
Ah, 'twas a perilous part
To play, of the prudent, eager-loving subject,
Entered so deep into a plot like this
Just for his master's sake. He's an awkward gift
Of divination, and beyond all doubt
He loved Sejanus. Nothing would convince him
But very proof itself. My lord, I hope
In all of this I did my duty to you ?

CALIGULA.

My friend, you have done well, and know that
    Gaius
Is not ungrateful.

CHÆREA.

What are the latest orders ?

CALIGULA.

That I should meet you here to-night and him,
Just as he wrote to me he wished, and then,
When I have seen *he* still is unaware,

Leave Rome at once and go back to the Island.
You will stay here. Have you not seen *him* yet?

CHÆREA.

I was prevented. I stay here? For what?

CALIGULA.

I cannot tell you. Macro and Artaxerxes
Are on the Island with the Prince.

CHÆREA.

Then nothing
Is done to-night? I do not understand.
Where shall I stay? Here with Sejanus?

CALIGULA.

No:
Depart with me and wait for orders in
The Palatine.

CHÆREA (*aside*).

Accursèd ass! But give me
To screw his head off!

CALIGULA.

Ho, what's that?

CHÆREA.

The guard.
[*At the balcony.*
See, there they come.
[*Soldiers marching behind through the
gardens.*

CALIGULA.

I do not like the moonlight :
It gives a ghastly look to things, like Hades.
My father Germanicus was prince of soldiers
Of all Rome ever had, and made the legions
Unconquerable as he was. How they march !
O, I was born with the trumpet in mine ears !
I wore a little pair of soldiers' shoes
When first I walked, and they called me Pretty
    Caligula.
I am all a soldier. In the deep tree shadow,
Their arms shine mildly like pure molten silver,
But now, see in the moonlight how they flash.
Ha, ha, ha !

[*Enter* SEJANUS.

SEJANUS.

What maniac's that
Laughing outside? Ah, thou, Chærea ? Aelia
Said thou wert come. What kept thee yester-
    day ?

CHÆREA.

In just a moment ! (*To* CALIGULA.) Lord
    Gaius——

CALIGULA.

Hi, hi, there !

Right wheel! round, round! Why, what—what
    is't, Chærea?

Sejanus? Good. (*Comes in.*) With all due
    gravity,

My lord, I have to tell you all is well.

SEJANUS.

That is good news. But you look pale and ill.

CALIGULA.

I am not quite myself to-night. I smell
Everything sickly, and my head's going round.
I saw the Prince at noon. Are we quite ready?

SEJANUS

Another speeding night shall see the moon
Sail upward in refulgence to the shout
Of Rome and the wide waiting world behind—
"Hail, Gaius, hail, hail, Cæsar, Imperator!"

CALIGULA.

And, since I am a god, yes, I *will* hail,
And lighten and thunder also.

CHÆREA.

             Ah, ha, ha!

CALIGULA.

I think it looks somewhat like rain. The moon
Is new and the old moon is lurid-rimmed.

CHÆREA.

And yet do many men asseverate

That, when the old moon in the young moon's
    breast

Is pale-rimmed with a yellow sickly look,

It means fine weather ?

CALIGULA.

          They contradict themselves.

Why should the frail moon and the short-houred
    stars

Be fatal to us more than the mighty earth

Or the reverberate sea, flouting the sun ?

There is an equal potency in all

Of Nature's signs if we could only find it.

SEJANUS (aside).

The fool has flashes of sense, astonishing changes

That almost make one dream he plays a part.

CHÆREA.

Profoundly true, my lord, profoundly true.

SEJANUS.

This afternoon I met Antonia.

She gave me one strange look, and passed along.

I do mistrust that woman. No letter came

From her to the Prince of late ?

CHÆREA.

> None, I am sure.

CALIGULA.

I think I will go down into the garden,
And talk with the soldiers.   So good-night,
  Sejanus.

SEJANUS.

Good-night, sire.

CALIGULA (*to* CHÆREA).

> You will find me by the cedar.

Do not be long.   I wish to start soon.

[*He goes out by the balcony and crosses the
  gardens.*

SEJANUS (*with* CHÆREA, *laughing*).

> Well ?——

CHÆREA.

Well, dead he will be tolerable.

SEJANUS.

> Pay him

No heed.   How go things ?   What's thy last
  report ?

CHÆREA.

All things are as they should be.

SEJANUS.

> And my ripe plum,

Electra ? Had she any pretty message ?
She says she always feeds men when they're
  hungry.

CHÆREA.

When in the bed-chamber we talked together,
In the villa at Misenum, and spoke of you,
She looked at the state-couch like a small house
And, laughing, said : "Well, there is lots of
  room !"

SEJANUS.

What a woman, Chærea ! Bad boy, thou hast
  made me shiver.

CHÆREA.

She had her doubts of Macro.

SEJANUS.

Doubts of Macro ?
A surly tongue-tied lout, Tiberius' hod-man,
Good but to lend a lean, lascivious wife
To my cracked, fellow boy-priest, our prince of
  boots !
But Artaxerxes is a different man.
For him I am uneasy all night long.
I almost wish we'd made him one of us.
What of him ? Didst thou mark ?

CHÆREA.

Absolute ignorance.

SEJANUS.

If so, we're safe.   I'll meet thee past the Gates
At dawn.   The troops concentrate by midnight,
And the city's ours.   If thou hast done as well
At the Isle, Tiberius is the mouse in the trap,
And we shall forthwith drop him in the bucket
And let him drink his fill down at the bottom.
Chærea, son, thou yet shalt sit with my girl,
And, Emperor by Empress, sway the state.

CHÆREA.

We yet may see it.

SEJANUS.

Keep good watch on Gaius.
Our stalking-horse is vital matter to us,
Till the game is down.   Were Macro not a dolt,
His wife might spice her vinegar lips with peril.
Till dawn, at the Gates, farewell !

CHÆREA.

Till dawn, at the Gates !
[*He goes out.*

SEJANUS (*at the balcony*).
Stars, myriad stars that jewel all the night,

And thou, fair-shadowed crescent, their pure
    queen,
Behold me, and ye powers and unknown gods,
That not as others, scornfully elate,
I seize this helm of things, I call Rome mine !
No, though I place beside the name Augustus
Sejanus, as proud a name ! (*Returning.*) I do
    remember
Once, a small truant, I saw the chariot races.
    [SOLDIERS *moving in the gardens, gathering*
        round the house.
There was one man who, quiet, humble, calm,
Held in his horses. He, when off they flew,
Skirted the others clearly to the goal,
And rounded furthest. Then, his face to home,
Taking a swerveless way, he loosed them out
Full to their stretch, and with an upraised face
And smile serene drove in his unstrained steeds,
Victor beyond all call ! The shrieking crowds
Were nothing to him, and Augustus' self
The paymaster of the gods !
            SOLDIER (*within*).
Who comes ?
           MACRO (*within*).
        A friend.

SOLDIER.

Stop, friend, and give the word.

MACRO.

White-suited Faith !

SEJANUS.

I'm sure I know that voice.

SOLDIER (*within*).

The counter-word ?

MACRO.

The Prince's Fortune.

SOLDIER.

Well,

No more ?

MACRO.

Yes, a Good Omen.

SOLDIER.

Pass along.

[MACRO *mounts the staircase and enters
behind.*

MACRO.

Hum, no one ?

SEJANUS.

Macro !

MACRO.

It is I, my lord.

SEJANUS.

What do you here?

MACRO.

I have a letter for you ;

'Tis from the Prince.

[*Sounds within*, SOLDIERS *advancing*.

SEJANUS (*reading*).

Hi, hi. 'Tis a fine night.

MACRO.

Yes, a fine night.

SEJANUS.

I thank you for the letter.

How did you learn the passwords?

MACRO.

I have here

A further warrant to you.

SEJANUS.

The Prince's signet?

I will obey. I pray you come with me.

[*Sounds below*.

SOLDIER (*within*).

Help! Help!

MACRO.

Help? Why, I think the help is come.

SEJANUS (*on the balcony*).
What, soldiers? treason?   Ho, I smell it out !
                                    [*Comes back.*

MACRO.
No, do not touch that sword.   'Tis better there
Upon the table.
                          [*Enter* SOLDIERS *behind.*

SEJANUS.
            I am in the toils !
These are strange faces.   What do you here, my
      men ?

MACRO.
I pray you to be seated.   Look, my lord.
                          [SOLDIERS *at both doors.*

SEJANUS.
The amphitheatre, it seems, is full.
                          [*Enter a* SECRETARY, *in white.*
Enter, White-suited Faith !

MACRO.
                          Put out the lamps.
Light those two torches.
      [*Enter* ARTAXERXES, *with* TIBERIUS *dis-
      guised.*

SEJANUS.

What is this mummery?

ARTAXERXES.

It is your trial.

(*Seated*, *to* SECRETARY).   Begin.

SEJANUS.

Why, that, I see, is Artaxerxes . . .

Artaxerxes!

ARTAXERXES.

The clerk is bidden begin.

SECRETARY (*reads*).

The charges 'gainst Sejanus are fourfold,
But all are to one purpose—treachery
Unto the Prince.

SEJANUS.

Ridiculous!

SECRETARY.

First, it is charged
That he did compass and achieve the death
Of the Prince's son adoptive and his heir,
Germanicus.

SEJANUS.

Ye gods!

SECRETARY.

                    And this he did
By poison.   Furthermore, since he well knew
Augusta, the Prince's mother, ever strove
Against Germanicus, for love of Drusus,
The Prince's son, he laid this to her charge
Through Piso and Plancina, her close friends.
Then, that he caused this Piso to be slain.

ARTAXERXES (*giving paper to* SECRETARY).
The proof of this is here.

SECRETARY.

Augusta thus : " *I do declare that Sejanus,*
commander of the Pretorian Guards, confessed
to me that by his agents he had compassed the
death of Germanicus in Syria, in this manner,
as he said, working in mine interests and those
of my son, the Prince, and my grandson, Drusus.
I do declarē that I never sought to put the odium
of this deed on to Piso and Plancina, his wife.
—AUGUSTA."

SEJANUS.

A clumsy forgery, a palpable, stupid forgery !

SECRETARY.

The Prince thus : " *Sejanus accused Augusta*

*of the death of Germanicus through Piso.
Sejanus undertook the death of Piso in conse-
quence.*—TIBERIUS."

[*To* SEJANUS.

Here are the letters, my lord. Be pleased to
    examine them.

ARTAXERXES.

The proof is good. Pass on to the third charge.

SECRETARY (*reads*).

The third charge is that, once again by poison,
He slew the Prince's son.

ARTAXERXES.

                The proof is here.

SECRETARY.

Livilla, wife of Drusus, the Prince's son, thus :
"*I confess that I was guilty of adultery with
Sejanus. I confess that at his instigation I
poisoned my husband, Sejanus promising to
marry me on his adoption by the Prince. I
confess also that I was aware of the poisoning
of my brother Germanicus by the order of
Sejanus.*—LIVILLA."

SEJANUS.

I cannot see in such a light as this.

L

ARTAXERXES.

The proof is good.   Pass on to the fourth
    charge.

SECRETARY.

The fourth charge is that by his practices
He tampered with the Guards : that at this hour
He aimed to seize on Rome and the Prince's
    person.

SEJANUS.

The proof, the proof !

ARTAXERXES.

                        The proof is here.
                        [*Enter* CHÆREA *behind.*
                                Behold ;

He has confessed.

SEJANUS.

    Chærea !

CHÆREA.

                        The game is up.

SEJANUS.

I say this is all false !   I do appeal
Unto the Prince !

CHÆREA.

    I'd say, appeal more loudly.
Artaxerxes cannot hear you.

SEJANUS.

False, all false !
The Prince knows well I love him.   I appeal
Unto the Prince.

TIBERIUS (*discovering himself*).

The Prince ?—The Prince is here !
[*The lights are lit and the others all go out.*
Sejanus.

SEJANUS.

Sire ?

TIBERIUS.

Hast thou no word to say ?
Hast thou no word to bid me not believe
The man I loved and trusted was a traitor ? . . .
What, not one word ?

SEJANUS.

Sire, not one word.   'Tis true.
I am a traitor.

TIBERIUS.

Tell me ; I'm fain to learn.
How did you fool one that's not yet a child,
To take you for his soul ?

SEJANUS (*kneeling*).

Sire, pardon me.

TIBERIUS.

You saved my life once.

SEJANUS.

I ask not for mine.

TIBERIUS.

Thou heldst me in thine arms. Open thy
    breast !   [*Draws the sword.*
I'll hack thy heart out !

SEJANUS.

Strike !

TIBERIUS.

No, no, no, no !

For I have yet something to question you.
That you should lust for power, miserable fool,
And with that lust forget your honesty,
I'd pity and I'd pardon. Dost thou know
Electra's dead ?

SEJANUS.

Electra ?

TIBERIUS.

Didst thou love her ?

Rise up, rise up. For I would hear, I say,
How thou hast learned to fool such men as I.
Have I no wits ? Mine eyes behold the stars.

I hear some sounds. I smell a rose. These hands
Can feel and catch and clutch.

                  [Takes him by the throat.

       SEJANUS.

               Kill—kill me, then !

       TIBERIUS.

No, no, I will not kill you. Only tell me
Why need you shame my bed ? To take my power,
To take my life, was not that, say, enough
But you must also foul me ? You knew I loved her.
Why must you shame her ?

       SEJANUS.

        'Tis not true. I could not.

       TIBERIUS.

Do not say that, for fear I torture thee—
Leave thee upon a cross to rot in the sun,
Or with a stake thrust through thee, or how else
I'll ponder in my leisure, but be sure
Thou shalt die slowly. Therefore unsay that !
Was it a longing for her night and day ?

Or but the pricking of one moment's lust
That could not wait another ?   No, I think
It was because you'd have me fooled and fouled,
The two together, and despise me quite ! . . .
What shall I do with him ? (*At the balcony.*)
 O Rome, Rome, Rome,
Thou harlot-horror of hell, corrupter of all,
I never dreamed to look on thee again,
But be sure,
If ever from this hour I see thy face,
'Twill be to watch thee flaming and thy flames
Quenched in hot blood. (*Returning.*) Sejanus,
 fare you well.
What you shall suffer, suffer manfully,
I do demand it.   Let the dunghill flies
Believe it was at least no coward whom
I loved and trusted.   As for me, behold
I am the first of those that all these things
Shall lash to madness.   What I'll do, I'll do—
Be what I'll be, and let the bloat bugs buzz.
Farewell !

   SEJANUS.
  Sire, sire, I do not ask for pardon :
Punish me as 'tis just.

You tempted me with all the world for bait,
And I was but a man.   Will you forgive?
I was not traitor always.

TIBERIUS.

                            Ha, what know I?
White-suited Faith !   The Prince's Fortune !
    Ho,
Guards, guards, guards !
    [*Re-enter* MACRO *and* SOLDIERS, TIBERIUS
        bassing through them.
    MACRO (*to the* SOLDIERS, *pointing to the doors*).
By there !   [*They go out.*

SEJANUS.

What is your pleasure ?   Do I go with you ?

MACRO.

Not so.   You stay.

SEJANUS.

                    I have a favour, sir,
To ask you.   May I see the great Chærea ?

MACRO.

He is not here.   He is gone.

SEJANUS.

                            I am well served.
Tell him I told you so. May I see my daughter ?

MACRO.

I'll send her to you.   You have little time.

[*He goes out.*

SEJANUS.

So, the race is run,
I am one of the idlers, and the good gods laugh !
I have too oft, I think, faced Death to fear
When now he faces me.   Ambition, power,
Are over for me for ever.   I am sped.
O what a fiery abyss behind !   I have done
Terrible things : women, and men and children,
Love, honour, all true things have been to me
But symboled counters in life's gambling-hell.
I have spent all my skill and reach to this—
To be a counter too, and the good gods laugh !
Dreams, dreams, and still but dreams !   Helpless
       and hopeless
Bewilderment confuses each with all,
And death, is that the waking? Dreams, dreams,
       dreams !

[*Re-enter* AELIA.

AELIA.

Father !

SEJANUS.

My child.

AELIA.

What is it that has happened ?
We are all prisoners.

SEJANUS (*holding her*).

Dear, thou dost not know
How thou art like thy mother.   I could think
This was the night, years, years and years
    ago, . . .
It was at night I won her, at the eve,
And that was when I lost her.   I came to her,
And found the nurse asleep, and she had called.
And then I knew that she was leaving me.

AELIA.

Father, dear father !

SEJANUS.

That was in another lifetime
Past, gone for ever !   Child, since then my days
Have dallied with the Furies, and at last
Their whips are round my shoulders.   Shall I say
I've played the insane gambler, I whose soul
Seemed all for happy quiet, since I lost
The pole-star of my life ?   It would seem so.

AELIA.

Thou hast done nothing but be ever good
And kind and gentle.

SEJANUS.

Do not make me laugh !
I have been loved and trusted and a traitor.
I have been honoured, and a murderer.
Thou wert a running sunny babe of three
When first Tiberius called me comrade, friend,
Co-operator in his world-wide work·
Of peace and power for all.   And I was loyal.
I was not traitor always.   Then Augusta,
Livia, the old stealthy wolf-bitch, tempted me.
Germanicus we poisoned ; the brave wife
We had poisoned too, but she escaped us thrice.
Next we slew Piso for the murderer,
And I accused Augusta, and she fell.
She died two years ago, but found a hand
To drive the venomed arrow to my breast.
I should have guessed it.   Then we poisoned
      Drusus,
I and his wanton wife.   Last, we drove out
The second Agrippina and her sons,
Nero and the other, while for Tiberius

We plotted and slew Gallus, him who married
Empty Vipsania. Lastly with Chærea——

AELIA.

I know it, father.

SEJANUS.

I and he together
Plotted for absolute empire, using as mask
That wise, mad, brat, beast and buffoon, young
    Gaius.
Chærea has betrayed me. All is lost.

AELIA.

How have I dreamed these years ! Thou dost
    not say
Such hideous things are true.

SEJANUS.

And there is worse.
To have his glittering brainless butterfly
Electra spy on him, I shamed her. O,
We are all liars, false and lecherous.

AELIA.

This is past hearing ! But Chærea—he——

SEJANUS.

Chærea's the double traitor who betrays
The oath of honour and dishonour and all

That goes with both. Yet, when thou seest the
    man,
Tell him that I forgave him. We are all here
Contemptible wretches.

AELIA.

        I will never see him !

SEJANUS.

Now, child, thou seest what thy father is.

AELIA.

O father, father, better to have died !

SEJANUS.

Ah, I was ever selfish. Poor, poor girl !
Didst thou love him, then ?

AELIA.

      No, no, I never loved him :
It was another !

SEJANUS.

I will entreat the Prince——

AELIA.

       Entreat ? Nay, father,
Entreat we nothing. Are we to be killed ?

SEJANUS.

I am.

AELIA.

That is we, for I am one with thee.

[*Re-enter* MACRO.

MACRO.

By the Prince's orders I am bidden take
This lady hence.

AELIA.

You will not do it, sir.
I am sure you will not. We are vowed to death,
Father and daughter.

SEJANUS.

Had I won the throw,
Girl, thou hadst been an empress !

MACRO.

I am bidden take you.

SEJANUS.

Thou must leave me.

AELIA.

No :

Thou art mine all ! I have nought left but thee.

MACRO.

I am bidden take you.

AELIA.

If you take me, take me
Unto the Prince.

MACRO.

These are vain, foolish words.
It is the Prince's pleasure that all three
Perish apart.

AELIA.

All three ?   My brother !   Father,
He too is taken ?   Must he perish too ?

MACRO.

He, too, is taken.

SEJANUS.

All that he must suffer,
He'll suffer justly and as a brave man should.
He, too, is guilty.   (*A shriek within.*)   What a
    cry was that !   [*Sounds within.*
Some one is slain.

MACRO.

Some soldiers they are stabbing.
You'll see them presently as we go down
Through the palace gardens.

                    [*Re-enter three* SOLDIERS.
Laco, the lady.   Take her hence.

AELIA (*snatching out a soldier's sword, but
            is disarmea*).

                    Ah, ah !

May I not even die ?   But do you think
A Roman woman cannot die without
That steel of yours ? Father, farewell. 'Tis over
Soon.   (*To* MACRO.)   I am ready.

MACRO (*to* SOLDIER).

Loose her.   She will go.

[AELIA *and* SOLDIERS *go out.*

MACRO (*on the balcony*).

Come up !

SEJANUS.

And these, these suffer for my sake !

[*Re-enter* SOLDIERS *behind.*

MACRO.

You come this way.   [*Trumpets and shouts.*

SEJANUS (*going*).

Is that for victory?

MACRO.

The plot is ended.   All the heads are down.

[SOLDIERS *seen in masses behind, brandishing*
swords.

SOLDIERS (*within*).

Ave, Cæsar, Imperator ! Ave, Cæsar, Imperator !

(THE SCENE CLOSES.)

ACT V.

Misenum.   Room in TIBERIUS' *villa.   Window
at left, looking out over the sea.   Curtain
behind, shutting off the dining-room.   Sun-
set.* TIBERIUS, ELECTRA.

TIBERIUS (*waking*).

What is this ?   The sea is one blue plain :
The sky one cloudless, rain-washed vault and
　　blue.
Day's luscious dreams are best. . . . Thou hast
　　the trick
Of the sense-soothing touch.   Some day perhaps,
When I am gorged with blood of venomous men,
I'll watch thine dripping in a golden bowl.
Now will she sing.   The white, full, flabby
　　throat
Swells with the song-throb. Ah, my fatted
　　nightingale !

ELECTRA (*singing with the cithara*).

O when the feast is set,
And the lamps are lit :
When the bowls with the wine are wet,
And the wreaths and fumes of the spices meet,
And the garlands of roses are sweeter than sweet
With the odour of it—
O when the feast is set,
And the lamps are lit !

TIBERIUS.

What magic hast thou, O thou rose o'erblown,
So fair a rosebud once, that thy rank soul
Yet holds some morning dew and colour in it ?

ELECTRA.

O when the eyes are bright,
And love is awake :
When low she breathes, the voluptuous night,
And the love-drawn fingers meet,
And the lips of lovers are sweeter than sweet,
And their faint hearts quake—
O when the eyes are bright,
And love is awake !

TIBERIUS.

For magic hast thou that thou art not dead,
But livest yet to tooth and fling away

M

And sip and spill men's fruits and weary wines.
Sejanus trusted thee.   So did Tiberius.
And both of them were fools.   Do we trust
    sparrows ?
They'll wanton in the shrubs, and for a cherry
Tell all our secrets !   Surely, now, thine age
Counts to the half of my Tithonus years,
Those living deaths I die and live each day.

ELECTRA (*playing*).

Phœbus is lord of the sea . . .
    Phœbus . . . Phœbus . . .
Where did I hear that song ?   La, la, la, la.
My dear, tell me where did I hear that song ?
    Phœbus is lord of the sea—
La, la, la, like that.   I'm sure I've heard it.

TIBERIUS.

Thou heardest it, maybe, from near a shrub.
The ladies in white robes sang it in the temple
Among the marble pillars.   She who sang it
Was a great tall lady with red, burnished hair
And a pale beautiful face.   It is all gone now.

ELECTRA.

O yes, yes, I remember it !   Isn't it strange
That I forgot it ?

TIBERIUS.

Well, it were more strange
Hadst thou remembered it. . . . " There shine
   on earth
No sea-span brighter than love-luring Baiæ,"
Horatius says.   And here the Romans swarm,
And flutter, and breed, and buzz, and call me
   " wicked,"
The wicked Prince over at Capreæ there—
Over at Capreæ there, past the coral rocks
In the dense vine wood.   And they then, sweet
   souls,
Will tell their tales of all the filth I do,
And it is filthy enough even for your moral
Ladies and Roman lords and for their friends,
The " philosophic republicans " who've the mange
And would have no hides scratched except their
   own,
Rotten with envious virtue. . . . Macro delights
   me.
He has the way of simple certainty.
He will go far, as far as he shall choose,
Just far enough, no farther.   Artaxerxes too.
They turn their faces from me now elsewhither.

Augustus told me once I lacked the knowledge
Into men's beings, but that comes with age,
Like flavour to the wine. . . . Electra, child,
What thinkest thou of Enna?

ELECTRA.

What do I think?
She has nice arms, but both her wrists and
        ankles
Are wooden-shaped.   Her eyes are big enough,
But the right squints a little.   She paints too
        much:
Her eyebrows are like pitch.   She's very thin.

TIBERIUS.

How speaks she?   Well?   Has she a ready wit?

ELECTRA.

Some men think so, who like a woman to look
As always kissing them.   To me she's coarse.
To see a woman so ready—that disgusts me.

TIBERIUS.

Ah, it disgusts thee?   How about her hair?

ELECTRA.

Well, it is long, and it would seem it's thick,
But it's all hanks like wool, and rough, and rank.

TIBERIUS.

What of her shape ? I'm half blind.

ELECTRA.

O my dear,

How canst thou say so ? She is like a knife.

TIBERIUS.

She is Egyptian. She smacks of the Nile.

ELECTRA.

Then I am glad I smack of somewhere else.

TIBERIUS.

The tempest is allayed now. We will cross
By morning over to the Island. I feel
Most dull and drowsy.

ELECTRA.

Well, I think that Gaius
Is a tiresome fool. She sits upon his knee,
And scrapes his hair before her husband and all.
He is quite indifferent. I don't think it's decent.
Her front teeth, too, are going.

TIBERIUS.

Wilt thou think so,
When he is Prince ? . . . And what will Gaius
    do,
When he is Prince ? Nay, nay, assuredly,

He'll have his purpose in this world of ours.
When he forgets his cowed and puling spirit,
He has at least in him the lust to rend,
And I have given him what he'll ease it with.
It makes me angry when they say it all
Is empty, idle torment.   Never think—
No, never think but that this work of ours
Shall have its crown yet and its throne, despite
Those harlots and their paramours at Baiæ !

ELECTRA.

Thou'lt make thyself quite ill.   Be not so angry.

TIBERIUS.

Julius, Augustus, yea, Tiberius,
Come not to live, to suffer and to slay,
To be the austere speech of the dumb earth,
Crying for vengeance, sick with hope of rest,
For a mere nothing. We are what we are made,
But something of it we have made ourselves,
Ruling the flood that bears us.   There is work
Greater to do than praise or blame of fools
And the fame of the quidnuncs or the infamy,
And I have done it !   With these palsied hands
I've torn those weeds up—dragged these blood-
    stained stones

That clogged the mighty plan of Julius,
And proud foundations that Augustus reared
To hold their places for the age to be ;
And, though the temple never greet mine eyes
But happier men shall chaunt and worship in it,
I have my glory !   O by all the gods,
I count it something, something more than much,
To fell the savage forest, clear the way
Through all the toils and perils of baulked hell,
For those who follow. Think you all these years
That I have sat, sombre and cold and calm,
The Fate of Rome and all her vermin nobles,
Mowing them out in sheaf-fulls with the scythe
My hand directed with a swerveless mind,
A clear-eyed hate—these years, these silent years
Of gall and rumination and despair,
Bitterness consumed and despair vanquished,
Shall count as nothing ?   All my life's renounce-
    ments,
Happiness, peace, content, gentle delight,
Yea, and the last stab of accursèd Nature
Through thrice-accursèd man—the hoodwinked
    loss
Of friendship and all human love and faith,

Shall count as nothing ?   Hear me, deaf dumb
    blind
Compulsion that art God ?   I have no need
Of vindication more than Thou.   Such right
Is thine as mine, is mine as thine, for ever !
I alone comprehend thee.   Past all words
I reach to thee and hold thee and possess.
I pass from mortal limits.   I am god,
Power inscrutable !

ELECTRA.

              My dear, my dear,
Thou'lt kill thyself with coughing.

TIBERIUS.

                      Water, water !
I thank thee—a god thanks thee who has got
Pains in his belly and his booming head
Worse than Zeus had a-swell with Pallas Athene.
There, there !   Bring in the supper.   Go
    (ELECTRA *going*) and tell them
To draw the curtains back.   I suffocate.
Music !   I hate the clattering of the dishes.

    [*Music. The curtain is drawn, discovering*
        the dining-room with windows all along
        the back, looking out over the sea. Low

*couches in right and left corners, with
tripod between them. Slaves bring in
viands, fruits, amphorae, etc. Some strew
the floor with dyed sawdust and saffron.
The lamps are lit, swinging from the
ivory ceiling.*

And these, too, live and batten in the sun
Like dogs and the fleas on them, like cocks and
    cockroaches,
Untroubled by the vision of what shall be.
Were it not better so ?   Is not this life
Of isolated thought and endless effort
One great illusion and delusion ?   Yet
It seemed the one thing precious in the foul pit !
What shall ensue, the heart-weary growth of
    time,
I see before me.   Would I live to see
With these infallible eyes the eternal weeds
Clogging and fouling it, and the slimy toads
Squat on each thought turned deed, however
    great,
However noble ?   No.   Then wherefore stay ?
I know not.   Something prompts in Nature's
    brain

To fight the fight through to the quiet close.
Here they come.

    [*Re-enter* ELECTRA.   *Enter* CALIGULA, ARTA-
        XERXES, MACRO, *and* CHÆREA.

Lie round the table.   Artaxerxes, there
Upon my right.   Speak soft, though I am deaf.
Electra, on the left.   [*They take their places.*

               This is not, my friends,
A commisatio.   Eat light, drink little.
Business attends us.   Keep our wit for that.

          (*To* ARTAXERXES.)

Have you all the papers with you ?

          ARTAXERXES.

                    Yes, sire, all,
They cover more than the month.

          TIBERIUS.

                 Presently read them.

        (*To* HEAD SLAVE.)

Draw back that curtain from the window there.

        CHÆREA (*to* ELECTRA).

The air's delicious now ; do you not find it ?

          ELECTRA.

We cross in the morning.

          CHÆREA.

               Is it so arranged ?

TIBERIUS (*to* HEAD SLAVE).

When they've borne round the dishes, let them
  go,
If thou hast anything pure, bring it to me.

CHÆREA (*to* CALIGULA).

My lord, you have one of your bad headaches?

CALIGULA.

        No.

ARTAXERXES (*to* MACRO).

The fleet from Egypt has come safe to port.
I have just got the letter.

MACRO.

      That is well.

CHÆREA (*to* ELECTRA).

Look at our Macro.   He lies square and eats
Like a machine.   He has a good digestion.

ELECTRA.

How is your friend Enna?

CHÆREA.

      Enna's not my friend.

ELECTRA.

I thought she was.   He told Lord Gaius so.

TIBERIUS.

I have no taste for food.   It's all like earth,

And everything I drink is foul and treacly.
Begin the papers, Artaxerxes.   We
Can go on slowly through them.   Stop the
    music.   [SLAVES *go out.*

           ARTAXERXES.
Falcinius Trio——

            CHÆREA.
      That's Sejanus' friend.

           ARTAXERXES.
Falcinius killed himself upon the kalends.
His will is published, full of rank abuse
Of Macro, and he ends with insolent gibes
Against the Prince.

            TIBERIUS.
       Well, read it to the Senate.

          ARTAXERXES (*notes*).   .
Read to the Senate.

            TIBERIUS.
       They'll weep to hear me gibed.

          ARTAXERXES (*reads*).
The Consuls celebrate the Decennial Games.

            TIBERIUS.
Kill them.

          ARTAXERXES (*notes*).
      The Consuls to be killed.

TIBERIUS.

Go on.

ARTAXERXES.

Ruso——

TIBERIUS.

Who is Ruso ?

CHÆREA.

I believe, sire, that
Is the young democrat imperialist.
You smiled to hear he'd called himself so once
In the Comitia.

TIBERIUS.

Well, and what of Ruso ?

ARTAXERXES.

Aufidius Ruso swears Getulicus
Planned for his daughter to marry Sejanus' son.

TIBERIUS.

Getulicus ?   Let him cool his ardours, then,
In Pontus' extreme outpost.   In three days
To clear from Italy, or death.   Water !

[ELECTRA *gives him some.*

ELECTRA.

Kiss me !

ARTAXERXES.

To Pontus banishment—extreme outpost—three
Days' grace to clear from Italy, or death.

ELECTRA.

Getulicus has a *pretty* face !

CHÆREA.
                        He'll chance
To get it spoiled in Pontus.   Very like
He'll have his nose frost-bitten and scraped off
By this next year.

CALIGULA.
                But *Naso* lost his *toes !*

ELECTRA (*to* TIBERIUS).

I think this very stupid.   Tell Chærea
To hold his tongue.   I didn't speak to him.
No one can get a word with him.   He talks
As bad as a woman.

ARTAXERXES.
                Paconius——

ELECTRA.
                            I am going
To sentence the next one.   What is his name ?

ARTAXERXES.

Paconius, lady.   He has writ bad verse
Upon the Prince.

ELECTRA.

O !

TIBERIUS.

Each declare his sentence ;
Electra's to be final.

ELECTRA.

Yes, that will do.
Mine to be final.   Go on.

TIBERIUS.

Well, propound.
Chærea ?

CHÆREA.

Banishment, sire.

TIBERIUS.

Gaius ?

CALIGULA.

Impalement.

TIBERIUS.

Macro ?

MACRO.

A flogging.

TIBERIUS.

Artaxerxes ?

ARTAXERXES.

A fine.

TIBERIUS.

Tiberius ?   What then says Tiberius ?   O,
I say let him go free.   I've writ bad verse
Myself: for that one's friends plague one enough.
Electra ?

ELECTRA.
Strangle him.

TIBERIUS.
That is the woman !

CHÆREA.

Her first reward for crime is death ; her second,
A pin-prick ; and her third ?   That would be
    kisses.

ELECTRA.
Strangle him.

TIBERIUS.
And so be it.

ARTAXERXES.
Strangulation.

TIBERIUS.
Does that content thee ?

ELECTRA.
I will sentence another.

TIBERIUS.
One is enough.

ELECTRA.

I *will* sentence another !

TIBERIUS.

Take some more wine.

ELECTRA.

I *will*, I *will!* Be silent.

TIBERIUS.

Take some more wine.   That will be best.

(*To* ARTAXERXES.)

Go on.

ARTAXERXES.

Agrippa poisoned himself on the last ides
In the Senate.   He had hid it in his ring.

TIBERIUS.

He'd a good name.   Agrippa once, my friends,
Loomed world-huge on us.   He is gone.   We go,
And dwarf distortion memorises us
In abject shapes.   Pompeius, Julius,
They'll call their dogs by.   You may live to hear
Cats called Tiberius.   What is next ?

ARTAXERXES.

Arruntius
Opened his veins on the eve of the nones.

N

TIBERIUS.

             · Arruntius ?
That's sad. Perchance I clear them out too quick,
Our viperous gentlemen. They have one virtue,
For which these fools forgive a thousand vices.
They die well.   So Arruntius, too, is gone ?
Augustus said he alone was able and worthy
To take the empire.   Dead in his bloody bath !
That's sad. Go on. No, stop. I have a point—
An edict, Artaxerxes.   Put it down.
I will not have, I say I will not have
This kissing in the streets.   It is too treacly.
We all grow eunuchs.   Stop it with an edict,
And the severest penalties.   That does
For Antioch or Alexandria;
But not for Rome.

CHÆREA (*to* CALIGULA).
And Artaxerxes never so much as blinked
When he said eunuch !

CALIGULA.
              Do not speak so loud.

ARTAXERXES.
Edict—street-kissing—penalties.

TIBERIUS.

I hear

My snake. . . .

ELECTRA.

O the horrid thing, eugh, eugh !

TIBERIUS.

He died

Last night on the Island, I am told.   I wonder
Did any one kill him ?   Hey ?

CHÆREA.

He was very old

And feeble, sire.

TIBERIUS.

Well, so am I.   His head
Had a bald scurfy flatness on the top
Like mine.   I'll see to it to-morrow when
We cross.   I do not wish him to be buried.
Cram up the rest in a bundle, Artaxerxes.
I'm sick of listening. Have they found Thrasyllus?
Charicles is a pompous fool.   Let him come no
    more,
Fiddling my wrist to see if the blood beats
Feebly enough to. . . .   [*Falls back.*

CHÆREA (*to* ARTAXERXES).

Look, I think the Prince
Has fainted.

TIBERIUS (*muttering*).

Do you say Gallus is dead?
I must not have him killed.   I am not yet
Reconciled with him.   More than enough, sweet
    wife.

CALIGULA (*to* MACRO).

Fainted, or faint-head—drunk.

CHÆREA.

His mind has wandered.
He's thinking of his wife.

CALIGULA.

Which one?   We've all
So many wives, we know not which is which.

ARTAXERXES (*to* ELECTRA).

Speak to him.

ELECTRA.

I'm afraid.

ARTAXERXES.

Sire——

TIBERIUS (*muttering*).

Conscript Fathers,

I know not what to write to you, or how
To write it, may the gods and goddesses—
· And goddesses destroy me with a death
More miserable than that which daily I feel.

ARTAXERXES.

Sire, sire, shall we break up?
If you would have the sitting end at once,
Pray say so, or but only bend your head.

TIBERIUS.

Antonia? What of her? There is a woman,
O there's a Roman woman, my brother's wife!
I said : "I spare Livilla for your sake,
Though she has murdered my son and shamed
     his bed
With the toad Sejanus." She thanks my clemency,
And starves the brach to death !

ARTAXERXES (*to* ELECTRA).

                    You sing to him.
It may arouse him.

ELECTRA.

          The cithara !

              [ARTAXERXES *brings it.*
CALIGULA (*to* ARTAXERXES).

                    What is this
Next item ?

ARTAXERXES.

This, Lord Gaius ?   Nerva insists
On suicide and kills himself on the nones.

CALIGULA.

The nervous idiot !

TIBERIUS.

Rise.   I will go out,
Electra, come.   The cithara ?   Well, bring it.
Thy shoulder, Artaxerxes, and thine arm.
Good-night to you. Gaius, good-night. Chærea,
Be with us in the morning.   Macro, bid
Them clear the tables. Good-night, all, good-
   night.

CALIGULA *and* CHÆREA.

Good-night, sire,
   [TIBERIUS, ARTAXERXES *and* ELECTRA *go out.*
      SLAVES *enter and clear the table, close the*
      curtain and put out some of the lights.

CHÆREA (*to* CALIGULA).

He spoke once of Thrasyllus, did you note, sire ?
Is he come yet ?

CALIGULA.

Is he come, Macro ?

MACRO.

He is not.
Artaxerxes will manage him, if he should come.

CHÆREA.

What wants he with the man Thrasyllus?

CALIGULA.

Thrasyllus
Is an astrologer.   He was at Rhodes.

CHÆREA.

I never heard him speak of him.

CALIGULA.

Artaxerxes
Can tell us of him.

CHÆREA.

Artaxerxes scarce
Shows zeal, methinks, so zealously as he might.

CALIGULA.

Chærea, Artaxerxes has my sanction
In all he does.   His prudence is our safety.

CHÆREA.

Sire, be it far from me to dream to doubt
His loyalty.   He is your devoted servant,
As we all are.   But——

CALIGULA.

That suffices.   Macro,
Art thou quite sure that nothing goes amiss ?

CHÆREA (*aside*).
It will suffice for several when I have done !

MACRO.
Nothing.   The rumour that the Prince is dying
Is spread about.   People stand at the gates.
The soldiers talk of him as dead already.
I have everything in hand.   The new guard's set
In a few minutes.

CALIGULA.

Does Electra know ?

MACRO.
No more than Enna does.

CALIGULA.

No, I've not told her !
Thou sayest truly.   Women are better used
For what they cannot see.   Their flighty hearts
Have such revulsions of diseased regret.
Must I be with thee when it's done.   Is it best ?

MACRO.
Yes, it is best.   It is very simple and easy.

CALIGULA.

He used to be so strong.

MACRO.

He is not now.

CHÆREA.

What shall be done with her ?

CALIGULA.

With whom ?

CHÆREA.

Electra.

CALIGULA.

Kill her, Macro ?

[MACRO *shrugs his shoulders.*

CHÆREA.

In faith, she is somewhat frowsy.

[*Re-enter* TIBERIUS.

TIBERIUS.

O, you are still here ?   Gaius sees a ghost.
Am I so frightful, then ?   Chærea, go.
I do not like the face you wear to-night.

[CHÆREA *goes out.*

Go too, my Gaius.   Macro, sleep within.

[CALIGULA *and* MACRO *go out.*

The night-wind's everywhere like a woman's
wail.

Electra is asleep flat on her back,
Clucking her lips just as she did, no doubt,
After she'd sucked her mother's Athenian teats,
A greedy baby.   Sometimes I would sleep,
And take to wander. Sometimes I would wander
And take to sleep.

> [*Draws the curtain on the right and goes in.
> Moonlight entering by the windows on to
> the couch.*

I seem Augustus with a foundering brain.
'Tis grateful so to lay out all the limbs.
I am very old, look, very old and feeble . . .
Oft-times I sat and watched him as he thought,
My cold, calm, mild, ancient and resolute snake.
He's dead now. No more thinks he now, nor
    dreams,
Nor sleeps, nor wonders why he is alive
And what this dying is. That's the best sleep . . .
I pray you . . . Phœbus is lord . . . is lord of
    the sea.

> [*Re-enter* ARTAXERXES *with* THRASYLLUS.
> ARTAXERXES.

The Prince is sleeping. He has just closed the
    Council,

And sent us all away. The storm last night
Delayed our passage over to the Island.
He sat there in the dark and watched the
    lightnings
Flash from the sea. They frighted some of us.

THRASYLLUS.

The Prince is sleeping ? Sleeping ? Yes, even
    so !
I come too late. Why did I come at all ?

ARTAXERXES.

What do you mean, sir ? No, he is not dead.
The Prince is ill and worn out with affairs.

THRASYLLUS.

If he's not dead, better, better he were !
Look at that face and see how cruel time
Has lashed it with her serpents. Yet we know
He was a babe and lisped at a mother's knee,
And smiled and laughed life's first sweet speech
    —for this !
He was a boy, too, beautiful and brave,
With soul-fed eyes and lips of passion's light.
It was for this ! A youth, next, bred on thought
Wiser than twice his years could reckon for,
The day's young archetype. It was for this !

I knew him as a man, suffering, mature,
Unconquered, with the grandeur of the gods
Looking from out his winkless gaze and face
Olympian, equal to the very fell
Necessity that rules our race and him.

ARTAXERXES.

Yes, yes, he is worn out.   Our loads are heavy.
What is the end of all ?   What is the gain ?

THRASYLLUS.

He went to do the world's great work—to win
Justice and joy for pitiable men ; and I,
I whom he loved, I left him all alone,
Heedful of nothing but a coward content.
And he has his reward—inexpiable
Suffering and scorn and weariness and woe,
The everlasting human spectacle,
Men's stupid greed and base ingratitude !
And I, what have *I* found 'neath serene stars ?
Nought but insane conceit, childish self-love—
Frenzied delusion and a sickened soul.
O, we are filth with our fools' inscrutable goals !

ARTAXERXES.

Yet what else shall we do ?   What hold ? what
    seek ?

THRASYLLUS.

The Prince is sleeping. There is no happier
    word.
Speak we no further. Come, he yet may wake.
When that can never be, he shall be blessèd.

ARTAXERXES.

Be it as you please, sir, be it as you please !

       [ARTAXERXES *and* THRASYLLUS *go out.*

TIBERIUS.

O, I heard voices in the twilight groves,
And sad ghosts gazed. at me. Now all is still.
Sleep is the last and sweetest thing life leaves.
Wherefore, Thrasyllus,
Wherefore, my friend, I do entreat your presence,
For I would seem to have a need of you,
That I may think there's yet one soul on earth
Simple in truth, sweet in sincerity,—
If you will come, and if it matters. Matters ?
Naught matters. All things tend but the one
    way :
That's degradation and disease and death.
And we ? Of us who know it, 'tis the same.
He was a fool who said the coward dies.
The coward lives. Death is more fell than life.

It baffles thought, and whispers wordless dreams.
Yet hatred, lust, revenge are things of price?
Old bloody Marius, so thou snarlest there,
Glaring from the black shadow like a wolf?
What is it with my heart—my heart? Ho—ho,
Some brute has got my heart.

> [*Re-enter* MACRO *and three* SOLDIERS.

MACRO.

There! Now be quick.

> [*They attack* TIBERIUS *to strangle him. He
> lies still. Re-enter* CALIGULA.

CALIGULA.

How he stares and grins. Macro, I am afraid.
Let us go out. His eyes have a mad look.
O, I will be beneficent! O, O!

> [*Covers his face.*

MACRO.

Sire, I salute you foremost. Ave, Cæsar!
Now to present yourself to the troops and people.

> [CALIGULA *and* MACRO *go out.*

ELECTRA (*within, singing softly to cithara*).

> Phœbus is lord of the sea!
> All day long
> The sound of his praise goes up
> Radiant and strong!

FIRST SOLDIER.

And yon's the Prince.

[*Cithara playing.*

SECOND SOLDIER.

Why, look you, he stirs yet.

TIBERIUS.

Brother, the lads !   What lads to do the work !
Rome, Rome !   [*He dies.*

FIRST SOLDIER.

He's dead now.

SECOND SOLDIER.

He crowed like a cock.

FIRST SOLDIER.

Quick, put it straight. They come again. Quick,
quick !

[*Re-enter* ELECTRA.

ELECTRA.

O that the god of day,
The lord of the sea,
Would speak with his lips but one word
To——   [*Shrieks and falls.*
[*Re-enter* THRASYLLUS *as the* SOLDIERS *go out.*

THRASYLLUS (*by the body*).
Yes,—true.   It is the one, the wakeless sleep,
The blessèd sleep, the far, forgotten sleep !

> [*Murmurs within.*

It is well done when done. Farewell, my friend,
You are the world's friend now.   I loved too
 late.   [*He kisses* TIBERIUS.

[*Re-enter* CALIGULA, ARTAXERXES, MACRO,
  CHÆREA, SOLDIERS *and* SLAVES.

ALL (*to* CALIGULA).

Ave, Cæsar, Imperator !

THRASYLLUS.

Greater than Cæsar, greater than Imperator,
Third of the three who gave the world to Rome !
Ave—ave atque vale !

> [*They all incline in silence.*

UNWIN BROTHERS, THE GRESHAM PRESS, CHILWORTH AND LONDON.

www.ingramcontent.com/pod-product-compliance
Lightning Source LLC
Chambersburg PA
CBHW032010060726
47497CB00017B/2451